TOEIC

練習測驗（3）

LISTENING TEST

In the Listening test, you will be asked to demonstrate how well you understand spoken English. The entire Listening test will last approximately 45 minutes. There are four parts, and directions are given for each part. You must mark your answers on the separate answer sheet. Do not write your answers in your test book.

PART 1

Directions: For each question in this part, you will hear four statements about a picture in your test book. When you hear the statements, you must select the one statement that best describes what you see in the picture. Then find the number of the question on your answer sheet and mark your answer. The statements will not be printed in your test book and will be spoken only one time.

Statement (C), "They're sitting at a table," is the best description of the picture, so you should select answer (C) and mark it on your answer sheet.

1.

2.

GO ON TO THE NEXT PAGE

3.

4.

5.

6.

GO ON TO THE NEXT PAGE

Directions: You will hear a question or statement and three responses spoken in English. They will not be printed in your test book and will be spoken only one time. Select the best response to the question or statement and mark the letter (A), (B), or (C) on your answer sheet.

7. Mark your answer on your answer sheet.

8. Mark your answer on your answer sheet.

9. Mark your answer on your answer sheet.

10. Mark your answer on your answer sheet.

11. Mark your answer on your answer sheet.

12. Mark your answer on your answer sheet.

13. Mark your answer on your answer sheet.

14. Mark your answer on your answer sheet.

15. Mark your answer on your answer sheet.

16. Mark your answer on your answer sheet.

17. Mark your answer on your answer sheet.

18. Mark your answer on your answer sheet.

19. Mark your answer on your answer sheet.

20. Mark your answer on your answer sheet.

21. Mark your answer on your answer sheet.

22. Mark your answer on your answer sheet.

23. Mark your answer on your answer sheet.

24. Mark your answer on your answer sheet.

25. Mark your answer on your answer sheet.

26. Mark your answer on your answer sheet.

27. Mark your answer on your answer sheet.

28. Mark your answer on your answer sheet.

29. Mark your answer on your answer sheet.

30. Mark your answer on your answer sheet.

31. Mark your answer on your answer sheet.

PART 3

Directions: You will hear some conversations between two people. You will be asked to answer three questions about what the speakers say in each conversation. Select the best response to each question and mark the letter (A), (B), (C), or (D) on your answer sheet. The conversation will not be printed in your test book and will be spoken only one time.

32. What is the man concerned about?
- (A) Rising paper costs.
- (B) Noise in the office.
- (C) A parking area closure.
- (D) Poor mobile phone reception.

33. What does the woman suggest?
- (A) Using public transport.
- (B) Working from home.
- (C) Reschedule a meeting.
- (D) Finding a different supplier.

34. What does the man say he will do?
- (A) Contact a supervisor.
- (B) Go on a trip.
- (C) Assemble a team.
- (D) Participate in a training session.

35. What is the woman inquiring about?
- (A) A payment option.
- (B) A ticket upgrade.
- (C) A flight schedule.
- (D) A dinner reservation.

36. What does the woman say she needs to do at 5:00 p.m.?
- (A) Give a presentation.
- (B) Rent a hotel room.
- (C) Meet some clients.
- (D) Catch a connecting flight.

37. What does the man say he can do?
- (A) Cancel a reservation.
- (B) Take a later flight.
- (C) Hold a table.
- (D) Contact a client.

38. What is the purpose of the call?
- (A) To purchase some supplies.
- (B) To return some merchandise.
- (C) To make shipping arrangements.
- (D) To locate a missing item.

39. What does American M ask for?
- (A) A tracking number.
- (B) An inventory amount.
- (C) The location of a building.
- (D) The weight of package.

40. What does the woman say about the box?
- (A) It is larger than average.
- (B) It may have been damaged.
- (C) It is needed soon.
- (D) It is brightly colored.

41. Who most likely is the woman?
- (A) A journalist.
- (B) A caterer.
- (C) An architect.
- (D) A receptionist.

42. What does the woman say she wants to do while she waits?
- (A) Attend a lecture.
- (B) Take some photos.
- (C) See a special exhibit.
- (D) Have lunch.

43. What does the man give the woman?
- (A) A free membership.
- (B) An audio recording.
- (C) A floor plan.
- (D) A daily schedule.

GO ON TO THE NEXT PAGE

44. Where are the speakers most likely to be?
- (A) At a food market.
- (B) At a restaurant.
- (C) At a department store.
- (D) At a bank.

45. What does the man offer the woman?
- (A) A sample.
- (B) A menu.
- (C) A newsletter.
- (D) A shopping bag.

46. According to the man, what will happen next week?
- (A) Job applications will be accepted.
- (B) An item will become available.
- (C) Prices will be lowered.
- (D) A new location will open.

47. What does the woman mean when she says, "I can't wait!"?
- (A) She is late for an appointment.
- (B) She is running out of patience.
- (C) She is excited about the event.
- (D) She is reluctant to speak.

48. What is the occasion for the luncheon?
- (A) To make a presentation.
- (B) To celebrate a business deal.
- (C) To honor a retiree.
- (D) To introduce new employees.

49. What does the woman say?
- (A) She led the team that gave the proposal.
- (B) She had nothing to do with the proposal.
- (C) She played an important part in the proposal.
- (D) She will not be present at the proposal.

50. Who most likely is the woman?
- (A) A bank employee.
- (B) A security guard.
- (C) A marketing consultant.
- (D) A shop cashier.

51. What does the man say about the business?
- (A) It has a good selection.
- (B) It has convenient hours.
- (C) It has weekly discounts.
- (D) It is close to his home.

52. What does the woman suggest the man apply for?
- (A) A contest.
- (B) A loan.
- (C) An employment opportunity.
- (D A shopper rewards card.

53. What are the speakers mainly discussing?
- (A) An advertising idea.
- (B) A hiring decision.
- (C) A product test.
- (D) A recent sale.

54. What problem does the man mention?
- (A) A business is closed.
- (B) An invoice listed the incorrect amount.
- (C) An event was delayed.
- (D) An order was shipped on the wrong date.

55. What does the man agree to do by Thursday?
- (A) Turn in a report.
- (B) Revise a manual.
- (C) Create an agenda.
- (D) Give a presentation.

DENTON'S

DEPARTMENT STORE

DISCOUNT COUPON

15% off purchases of $400 or more

(00) 0 0123456 000000001 8

Coupon expires May 15

56. What is the man doing?
(A) Assisting a customer.
(B) Handing out coupons.
(C) Arranging some displays.
(D) Restarting a computer.

57. Look at the graphic. Why was the coupon rejected?
(A) It has expired.
(B) It was issued by another store.
(C) It must be approved by a manager.
(D) It is for purchases of $400 or more.

58. What does the man agree to do?
(A) Hold some items at the counter.
(B) Initialize the coupon.
(C) Authorize an additional discount.
(D) Call another staff member.

59. Why is the woman calling the hotel?
(A) To organize a conference.
(B) To confirm an address.
(C) To complain about a service.
(D) To change a reservation.

60. What does the man suggest?
(A) Taking a shuttle bus.
(B) Checking the hotel's website.
(C) Calling back at a later time.
(D) Staying an additional night.

61. What will the man ask the manager to do?
(A) Explain a policy.
(B) Provide a schedule.
(C) Authorize a discount.
(D) Change a restriction.

62. Why was the man's company contacted?
(A) To build a garage.
(B) To investigate a bad smell.
(C) To remove a tree.
(D) To install an appliance.

63. What does the man say he will do before returning tomorrow?
(A) Pick up supplies.
(B) Test some equipment.
(C) Hire extra workers.
(D) Talk to a manager.

64. What will the woman do on Monday?
(A) Call the man.
(B) Host an event.
(C) Paint a room.
(D) Send a payment.

GO ON TO THE NEXT PAGE.

REGAL AUDITORIUM
Admission Price (per Person)

University student $18
Group of 10 or more $20
Member $15
Nonmember $25

Frazier Mobile
Billing Statement: 06/23
www.fzrmobile.com

Equipment	FZR 9980 Silver 16GB GSM	$700.00
Service Plan	Diamond Unlimited (monthly)	$75.00
Warranty	Two-year Extended	$100.00
Sub-total		$875.00
Fees and Taxes/ State sales tax (8.75%)		$76.56
Total		$951.56

65. What type of event are the speakers discussing?
(A) A theater performance.
(B) A museum exhibit opening.
(C) A photography workshop.
(D) A live music concert.

66. Look at the graphic. What ticket price will the speakers probably pay?
(A) $15.
(B) $18.
(C) $20.
(D) $25.

67. What does the woman suggest the man do?
(A) Pay with a credit card.
(B) Rent some equipment.
(C) Leave work early.
(D) Call a coworker.

68. Who most likely is the woman?
(A) A store clerk.
(B) A real estate agent.
(C) A banker.
(D) A teacher.

69. What does the man ask about?
(A) Additional features.
(B) Online payments.
(C) Trade-in policies.
(D) Coverage area.

70. Look at the graphic. How much will be removed from the bill before taxes?
(A) $75.00.
(B) $76.56.
(C) $100.
(D) $700.

PART 4

Directions: You will hear some talks given by a single speaker. You will be asked to answer three questions about what the speaker says in each talk. Select the best response to each question and mark the letter (A), (B), (C), or (D) on your answer sheet. The talks will not be printed in your test book and will be spoken only one time.

71. Who are the listeners?
(A) Software developers.
(B) Legal assistants.
(C) Restaurant staff.
(D) Hotel managers.

72. What will the listeners do at the workshop?
(A) Develop goals for the upcoming year.
(B) Discuss customer feedback.
(C) Learn to use new software.
(D) Participate in role-playing activities.

73. What does the speaker expect will happen?
(A) Customers will write positive reviews.
(B) Sales volumes will increase.
(C) There will be fewer billing errors.
(D) Employees will work more efficiently.

74. Where does the speaker most likely work?
(A) At a real estate agency.
(B) At a law firm.
(C) At an insurance policy.
(D) At a warehouse.

75. What does the speaker say about the property?
(A) It has modern facilities.
(B) It is in a good location.
(C) It is large.
(D) It is not available.

76. What does the speaker ask the listener to do?
(A) Visit a Web site.
(B) Make an appointment.
(C) Apply for a loan.
(D) Return a phone call.

77. Who is the intended audience for the talk?
(A) Customers.
(B) Job candidate.
(C) Production workers.
(D) Managerial staff.

78. According to the speaker, where will the listeners go next?
(A) To the assembly floor.
(B) To the shipping department.
(C) To a training room.
(D) To a security office.

79. What are the listeners asked to do?
(A) Practice safety procedure.
(B) Sign a form.
(C) Turn in a job application.
(D) Use a security badge.

80. What type of business is Vestige Entertainment?
(A) A game developer.
(B) An electronic store.
(C) A weapons manufacturer.
(D) A wedding planner.

81. Why is there a delay?
(A) Some materials are not available.
(B) Machinery is being replaced.
(C) A price has not been determined.
(D) More product testing is necessary.

82. What are customers encouraged to do?
(A) Order items in advance.
(B) Check a Web site for updates.
(C) Compare specifications.
(D) Read consumer reviews.

GO ON TO THE NEXT PAGE.

WILLIAMS WILDLIFE RESCUE CENTER

83. Who is the talk intended for?
    (A) Nature photographers.
    (B) City officials.
    (C) New volunteers.
    (D) University students.

84. Look at the graphic. Which trail is closed to visitors?
    (A) North Lincoln Trail.
    (B) Cumberland Trail.
    (C) DeKalb Trail.
    (D) Dawson Trail.

85. What project is the Center participating in?
    (A) An annual clean-up day.
    (B) A program to plant more trees.
    (C) A series of seminars on wildlife conservation.
    (D) A research study on chimpanzees.

86. What will happen on April 22?
    (A) Mail service will be extended.
    (B) Paychecks will be issued.
    (C) A training session will be held.
    (D) Work schedules will be adjusted.

87. What are listeners asked to review?
    (A) A customs declaration.
    (B) A project timeline.
    (C) A customer survey.
    (D) An employee handbook.

88. What does the speaker say about the part-time employees?
    (A) They will receive a certificate.
    (B) They will be paid for extra time.
    (C) They are not included in a policy.
    (D) They must sign a tax form.

89. What is being announced?
    (A) An anniversary celebration.
    (B) A grand opening.
    (C) A renovation project.
    (D) A sweepstakes giveaway.

90. What will happen tomorrow morning?
    (A) An award will be presented.
    (B) A restaurant will serve free breakfast.
    (C) Stores will open early.
    (D) A design will be displayed.

91. According to the announcement, what is available at the information desk?
    (A) A schedule of events.
    (B) A brochure with coupons.
    (C) A map of the area.
    (D) A list of restaurants.

92. Why has the speaker called today's meeting?
    (A) To discuss the quarterly budget.
    (B) To clarify an assignment.
    (C) To finalize product designs.
    (D) To test a new product.

93. What has the company been asked to do?
    (A) Design a coffee table.
    (B) Create an advertising campaign.
    (C) Lower monthly costs.
    (D) Meet an earlier deadline.

94. According to the speaker, what will happen at the next meeting?
    (A) A demonstration will be held.
    (B) A competitor's product will be analyzed.
    (C) Proposals will be reviewed.
    (D) Materials will be rewritten.

TRAVEL EXPENSE REPORT

Name: Bob Colvin
Department: Sales
Date(s) of trip: October 12-13

Date	Amount	Description
10/12	$124.00	Round-trip economy class airfare (Phila. – Boston)
10/12	$45.86	Taxi from Boston Logan International to Camp Corp.
10/12	$77.29	Meal with client at Bosco's Restaurant
10/12	$15.50	Certified copies of signed contracts
10/13	$225.00	K Hotel Boston
10/13	$55.93	Taxi from K Hotel Boston to BOS

Total: $487.65

95. Why is the speaker calling?
(A) A meeting has been cancelled.
(B) A client has a question.
(C) A flight has been delayed.
(D) A receipt is missing.

96. Look at the graphic. Which expense needs to be documented?
(A) Airfare.
(B) Restaurant.
(C) Taxi.
(D) Hotel.

97. What does the speaker say she can do?
(A) Explain a process.
(B) Issue a check.
(C) Issue a receipt.
(D) Contact a supervisor.

CITY OF BELLEVUE
CITY COUNCIL AGENDA
August 23 7:00 p.m.

7:00-7:10   Welcome and introduction – Leigh Brawley, moderator

- Purpose of meeting – Tiffany Cheever, City of Bellevue mayor
- City of Bellevue, Office of Budget and Management – Ingrid Medina, city budget director
- Snohomish County Department of Transportation – Scott Rippertin, acting deputy

7:30-8:30   Public comment and open discussion – Leigh Brawley, moderator

98. What problem is the speaker addressing?
(A) Scheduling delays.
(B) Road congestion.
(C) Budget cuts.
(D) Tax reductions.

99. What did the city do in June?
(A) Conducted a study.
(B) Changed parking regulations.
(C) Held an election.
(D) Fired four police officers.

100. Look at the graphic. Who is the current speaker?
(A) Leigh Brawley.
(B) Tiffany Cheever.
(C) Ingrid Medina.
(D) Scott Rippertin.

This is the end of the Listening test. Turn to Part 5 in your test book.

GO ON TO THE NEXT PAGE.

READING TEST

In the Reading test, you will read a variety of texts and answer several different types of reading comprehension questions. The entire Reading test will last 75 minutes. There are three parts, and directions are given for each part. You are encouraged to answer as many questions as possible within the time allowed.

You must mark your answers on the separate answer sheet. Do not write your answers in your test book.

PART 5

Directions: A word or phrase is missing in each of the sentences below. Four answer choices are given below each sentence. Select the best answer to complete the sentence. Then mark the letter (A), (B), (C), or (D) on your answer sheet.

101. Jeff Dannon, the interim press secretary, will attend the news conference ------- Mayor Heffernan.
 (A) likewise
 (B) on behalf of
 (C) provided that
 (D) because

102. Same-day delivery can be scheduled ------- you place your order before 11:00 a.m. Eastern Standard Time.
 (A) if
 (B) for
 (C) yet
 (D) either

103. New York City's Director of Transportation said that the ------- challenge facing the city is overcrowding on public buses.
 (A) significantly
 (B) most significant
 (C) significance
 (D) to signify

104. Amid increasing -------, restaurant and bar owners have added innovative cocktails to their menus.
 (A) competitive
 (B) competitor
 (C) competition
 (D) competed

105. All ------- will take place at the Alpine Valley Music Theater.
 (A) performs
 (B) performances
 (C) perform
 (D) performer

106. ------- waste of raw material during production has caused profits to decline at the DuMont Chemical Company.
 (A) Vivid
 (B) Excessive
 (C) Unsure
 (D) Skilled

107. Foster-Brockton Industries seeks to recruit ------- staff and is committed to helping its employees develop their careers.
 (A) diversity
 (B) diversify
 (C) diverse
 (D) diversely

108. Neither the value ------- the contents of the shipment are accurately reflected on the invoice.
 (A) but
 (B) though
 (C) and
 (D) nor

14

109. Ms. Allen volunteered to assist at the front desk ------- she has no experience working directly with customers.
(A) so that
(B) or
(C) even though
(D) until

110. Although ------- of the new Jackson smart phones are available in stores, many of them can be purchased online.
(A) nothing
(B) none
(C) no
(D) no one

111. Martindale Financial is always ------- to consider qualified professionals who are interested in joining our organization.
(A) necessary
(B) possible
(C) useful
(D) willing

112. Dr. Sanchez intends to remodel the waiting room to make it more ------- for her patients.
(A) probable
(B) capable
(C) comfortable
(D) reachable

113. Because the President's statements were not quoted -------, the interview must be revised before publication.
(A) correcting
(B) correction
(C) corrects
(D) correctly

114. Jetson's line of patio furniture is popular because it is attractive and ------- priced.
(A) afforded
(B) affordability
(C) affording
(D) affordably

115. The artist revealed that the themes of his work are drawn ------- from his experiences growing up in Florida.
(A) ideally
(B) largely
(C) seemingly
(D) probably

116. The Hotel Florence's flexibility regarding check-in times is an ------- of its commitment to customer satisfaction.
(A) indicating
(B) indicative
(C) indication
(D) indicated

117. Some seats are still available in the third row for those who want a closer ------- of the performers.
(A) view
(B) sight
(C) watch
(D) show

118. Should we narrow the candidate list now, or do we do it ------- Ms. Yeager contacts the applicants' references?
(A) once
(B) then
(C) now
(D) just

119. Mr. Spangler ------- the keynote speech at the computer convention in Detroit.
(A) pursued
(B) implied
(C) delivered
(D) achieved

120. The maintenance department will ------- a test of the building's fire alarm system this morning at 10:15.
(A) install
(B) repair
(C) conduct
(D) acquaint

GO ON TO THE NEXT PAGE

121. The building contractors offered Selby Electrical the same contract terms ------- were offered to them last year.
(A) whose
(B) when
(C) that
(D) they

122. From fishing rods to rifles to camping gear, Toby's has the merchandise you need for any outdoor recreational -------.
(A) activated
(B) activating
(C) activity
(D) active

123. Bertz Transportation Co. is planning to add a dozen more hybrid-electric vehicles to its ------- fleet.
(A) rent
(B) rental
(C) to rent
(D) rents

124. An unusually large number of employees in the finance department retired last year, leaving six positions -------.
(A) invalid
(B) blank
(C) hollow
(D) vacant

125. When requesting reimbursement for travel expenses, be sure to ------- the signed claim form with your receipts.
(A) include
(B) includes
(C) included
(D) including

126. Government restrictions on the import of building materials were temporarily lifted ------- meet increased demand.
(A) in order to
(B) by means of
(C) for the moment
(D) as a matter of fact

127. Clear Mountain Apparel announced that it will release many new ------- in the coming year.
(A) itemize
(B) items
(C) item
(D) itemized

128. The events committee has ------- requested that Oakville Caterers provide the food for this year's holiday party.
(A) specifics
(B) specified
(C) specifically
(D) specified

129. Please update your account information ------- submitting your credit increase application.
(A) during
(B) around
(C) before
(D) within

130. Susie Richardson was named Best Emerging Reporter for ------- writing on the recent election.
(A) she
(B) her
(C) our
(D) their

PART 6

Directions: Read the texts that follow. A word or phrase is missing in some of the sentences. Four answer choices are given below each of the sentences. Select the best answer to complete the text. Then mark the letter (A), (B), (C), or (D) on your answer sheet.

Questions 131-134 refer to the following notice.

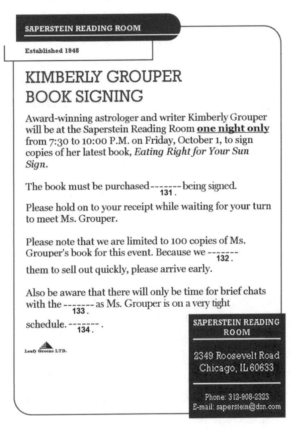

SAPERSTEIN READING ROOM

Established 1948

KIMBERLY GROUPER BOOK SIGNING

Award-winning astrologer and writer Kimberly Grouper will be at the Saperstein Reading Room **one night only** from 7:30 to 10:00 P.M. on Friday, October 1, to sign copies of her latest book, *Eating Right for Your Sun Sign*.

The book must be purchased ------- being signed.

131.

Please hold on to your receipt while waiting for your turn to meet Ms. Grouper.

Please note that we are limited to 100 copies of Ms. Grouper's book for this event. Because we -------

132.
them to sell out quickly, please arrive early.

Also be aware that there will only be time for brief chats with the ------- as Ms. Grouper is on a very tight

133.

schedule. ------- .

134.

Leafy Greens LTD.

SAPERSTEIN READING ROOM

2349 Roosevelt Road
Chicago, IL 60633

Phone: 312-908-2323
E-mail: saperstein@dsn.com

131. (A) regardless of
(B) except for
(C) prior to
(D) on behalf of

132. (A) had expected
(B) were expecting
(C) would have expected
(D) are expecting

133. (A) author
(B) publisher
(C) owner
(D) singer

134. (A) To order advance copies of Ms. Grouper's book, please contact Jerry at 334-3321
(B) To reserve a seat for the concert, please visit our website at www.saperstein.com
(C) To cancel an existing reservation, please press "0" on your touch tone key pad
(D) To schedule an appointment with an astrologer, email dave@saperstein.com

GO ON TO THE NEXT PAGE.

Support from the Web

"A time-tested method to grow a business is to create a Web presence," says Olivia McGee, owner of Euphoria, a women's clothing boutique.

When Ms. McGee started her business five years ago, she was convinced that having sufficient inventory and an ------- shop on
135.

a busy thoroughfare would be all she needed for success. ------- , her opinion
136.

has shifted since that time. "More and more customers were asking if my shop had a Web site, said Ms. McGee.

"Eventually, I began to realize that an online presence is becoming ------- ."
137.

Now Ms. McGee conducts much of her business from the Euphoria Web site, where customers can view merchandise, learn about special sales, ------- .
138.

135. (A) attraction
(B) attracts
(C) attracted
(D) attractive

136. (A) As a result
(B) Whereas
(C) Even if
(D) However

137. (A) confident
(B) apparent
(C) necessary
(D) accustomed

138. (A) but leave no impression on the customer
(B) and have their purchases shipped directly to their homes
(C) with everything you need to know about success
(D) to complete an international transaction

Dear Mr. Ferguson,

We appreciate your interest in the Berkshire Sales training seminars. Our sessions help companies to improve sales and increase the overall efficiency of their operations. Seminar ------- learn to apply the most
139.
effective sales and negotiation techniques in use today. Our company ------- the members of your sales team all the skills necessary to meet
140.
and surpass your performance expectations. -------. I have enclosed a
141.
schedule of the upcoming topics and dates ------- you to peruse.
142.

To receive more information, please email me at:

s_paulson@berkshiresales.com.

Sincerely,

Silvia Paulson

Sales Training Coordinator, Berkshire Consulting

---

139. (A) participating
(B) participants
(C) participate
(D) participated

140. (A) has taught
(B) be taught
(C) will teach
(D) is teaching

141. (A) The seminar will conclude at 5:30 p.m. Saturday
(B) The position will remain open until a qualified applicant has been hired
(C) The clearance sale will be extended throughout the month of July
(D) The training sessions are available online or in person at the location of your choice

142. (A) from
(B) across
(C) for
(D) past

GO ON TO THE NEXT PAGE

TABLA RASA
GRAND RE-OPENING

Megan and Chuck Monroe, the new owners of Tabla Rasa, invite you to join them for the restaurant's grand re-opening. The Monroes ------- major

143.

improvements to Tabla Rasa. The new menu, created by award-winning chef Gilberto Ruiz, features regional specialties ------- with innovative

144.

food trends. Chef Ruiz also has added an expanded selection of desserts using locally sourced produce. Diners at Tabla Rasa will be delighted to find excellent food combined with outstanding service in this fresh and exciting atmosphere. The redecoration ------- the dining

145.

room has introduced contemporary yet casual furniture and attractive indirect light. -------.

146.

143. (A) will make
   (B) make
   (C) have made
   (D) to make

144. (A) exchanged
   (B) integrated
   (C) recruited
   (D) afforded

145. (A) since
   (B) of
   (C) about
   (D) up

146. (A) Since last month, customers are not allowed to use laptops
   (B) The farmer will be on hand to pass out free samples
   (C) Reservations are not required but are recommended
   (D) Please hold and a representative will be with you shortly

PART 7

Directions: In this part you will read a selection of texts, such as magazine and newspaper articles, e-mails, and instant messages. Each text or set of texts is followed by several questions. Select the best answer for each question and mark the letter (A), (B), (C), or (D) on your answer sheet.

Questions 147-148 refer to the following e-mail.

From:	Elie Kravitz <eliekravitz@hoovergadgets.com>
To:	bobkelly@freelancer.com
Re:	Assignment
Date:	October 4

Dear Mr. Kelly,

We received your translation of the instruction manuals. We are very pleased with your work, so we will continue to employ your services.

To complete this assignment, we need your cooperation on a couple of things. First, as you finish each manual, please return the original document we gave you.

Meanwhile, you asked for your fee to be deposited directly into your account. Unfortunately, it seems that I have deleted the email message with your account number. Please send it again as soon as possible so that we can pay you for your work.

Thank you very much,
Elie Kravitz

147. What is the purpose of the e-mail?
(A) To offer assistance.
(B) To inform.
(C) To inquire about a fee.
(D) To ask for a phone number.

148. Who is Mr. Kelly?
(A) A translator.
(B) A teacher.
(C) A marketing specialist.
(D) A bank employee.

GO ON TO THE NEXT PAGE.

From:	Rex Grossman <g_rex@ymail.com>
To:	Customer Service <customerservice@wer.biz>
Re:	Subscription # 23238
Date:	May 3

I will be out of the country during the months of June and July, and thus, I'm requesting a suspension of my subscription to Weekly Economic Report magazine..

From my experience in previous years, it is my understanding that my subscription will be extended by these two months, which means that my subscription will not expire in November but in January of next year.

If this is not the case, please contact me by e-mail to clarify your current subscription policy.

As always, thank you for your efficient service.

Sincerely,
Rex Grossman

149. What is the main purpose of the e-mail?
(A) To cancel a magazine subscription.
(B) To ask that the delivery be stopped temporarily.
(C) To request a copy of a current issue.
(D) To report that some issues were not delivered.

150. What is suggested about Mr. Grossman?
(A) He was once a writer for the Weekly Economic Report.
(B) He is not satisfied with the customer service.
(C) He's planning a trip abroad.
(D) He decided to cancel the suspension.

Questions 151-152 refer to the following letter.

Quartz Digital Services
498 33rd Avenue #3B
San Francisco, CA 94121

May 30

Ms. Pamela Brooks
234 Buena Vista Terrace
Cupertino, CA 94572

Dear Ms. Brooks,

Thank you for your letter of May 25 inquiring about our services. QDS offers a full range of editing and printing services help with development of advertisements, informational posters and Web sites. I am enclosing our latest brochure with a price list. You will see that our rates are more reasonable than those of our competitors.

I look forward to hearing from you again.

Sincerely,
Jason Torrance
QDS
Sales manager

151. What is a service that Quartz Digital Services provides?
(A) Accounting.
(B) Training.
(C) Advertising.
(D) Printing.

152. What does Mr. Torrance indicate about Quartz's prices?
(A) They can be reduced for large orders.
(B) They are listed on the company's Web site.
(C) They are lower than those of other businesses.
(D) They depend on the customer's location.

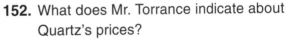GO ON TO THE NEXT PAGE

From:	All employees <staff@deerfield.com>
To:	Luke Pollard <lpollard@deerfield.com>
Re:	Avery Coonley Day Camp
Date:	May 1

Deerfield Outfitters Inc. will be helping Avery Coonley Day Camp prepare for the upcoming summer.

This nonprofit camp relies on Deerfield Inc. and other companies to keep its registration rates affordable in order to maximize the number of local children it can serve. The camp serves children aged six to twelve. Many of our own employees send their children to Avery Coonley. Our camp supply drive begins tomorrow. Large containers will be placed in the lobby of our headquarters. Arts and crafts supplies, board games, pool toys, and sunscreen are especially needed. Sporting equipment, such as tennis balls, baseballs, and baseball bats, would be appreciated as well. Donations will be accepted until May 31. If you would prefer to make a monetary donation, please give it to Chloe Sampson, Human Resources Department, Room 34.

Thank you in advance for supporting this wonderful camp.

Luke Pollard
Community Service Coordinator, Deerfield Outfitters, Inc.

153. What is the purpose of the e-mail?
(A) To organize a gift exchange.
(B) To offer a discount to a day camp.
(C) To recommend summertime activities for children.
(D) To solicit support for a local organization.

154. What would probably NOT be placed in one of the large containers?
(A) Colored pencils.
(B) Chess sets.
(C) Beach balls.
(D) Cans of food.

Regional Light Rail Service

Attention Passengers:

The Regional Light Rail Service has recently redesigned its Web site to offer a wider array of helpful information. The site (www.lightrail.com) now lists all fares and train schedules, including those for weekends and holidays. You can purchase or reserve tickets in advance through the Web site, find information about traffic delays on local roads, and get regional light rail maps to help you plan your travels.

Any delays or service interruptions will be posted on the site, which will be continually updated. In the rare event of a major service interruption on one or more train lines, our Web site will display time estimates for service to be restored.

We hope the enhanced Web site will make light rail travel even more convenient for you. We are always looking for ways to improve our site and our service. Please e-mail any questions or suggestions to info@lightrail.com.

155. What is the main purpose of the notice?
(A) To inform the public of the condition of local roads.
(B) To publicize recent changes made to a Web site.
(C) To notify travelers about upcoming changes in train service.
(D) To provide information on purchasing rail tickets.

156. According to the notice, what information is available on the website?
(A) Bus schedules.
(B) Service delays.
(C) Safety advice.
(D) Job openings.

157. How may passengers contact Metro Transit Rail Service?
(A) By calling an office.
(B) By sending an e-mail.
(C) By visiting an office.
(D) By taking a survey on the website.

GO ON TO THE NEXT PAGE.

From:	Mark Ellison <markellsion@apexauto.com>
To:	Jeff Bezos <jeffbezos@smail.com>
Re:	Your Inquiry
Date:	August 23

Dear Mr. Bezos,

In response to your previous e-mail regarding our Apex automobile parts, here is the related information on our repair service.

Repair and Replacement under Warranty

- Any replacement parts furnished at no cost to the purchaser in fulfillment of this warranty are guaranteed only before the original warranty expires.
- Apex guarantees for a period of 90 days from the date of shipment that each standard product shall be free of defects in material and workmanship. During this period, if the customer experiences difficulties with an Apex product and is unable to resolve the problem with Apex customer support, Apex headquarters should be notified. Upon receipt of the notification, we will ship a new unit to the purchaser by flat freight at Apex's cost.
- After 90 days, standard products will no longer be eligible for no-cost repair and replacement. Any service or repair beyond the warranty period shall be at Apex's rates.
- Custom-built products are NOT eligible for no-cost replacement under warranty.

I hope all of this is clear to you. Please feel free to contact me if you have any further questions. I will be more than happy to assist you.

Regards,
Mark Ellison
Apex Auto Product Support

158. What is the purpose of the e-mail?
(A) To clarify a policy.
(B) To confirm a purchase.
(C) To request product repairs.
(D) To introduce a product.

159. What is NOT stated in the letter?
(A) Apex will reimburse customers for shipping charges.
(B) Custom-built products will not be replaced free of charge.
(C) Only standard products are eligible for coverage.
(D) Products are guaranteed against material defects.

160. How are customers asked to first address difficulties with Apex products?
(A) By returning the product to a Apex store.
(B) By calling Apex headquarters.
(C) By contacting customer support.
(D) By requesting a replacement unit.

Questions 161-163 refer to the following Web page.

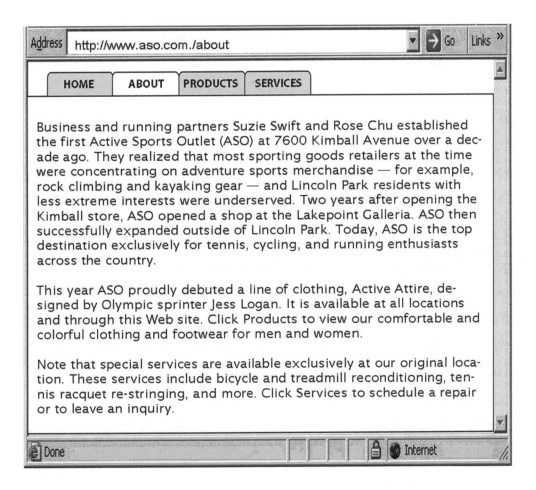

Address http://www.aso.com./about ▼ →) Go Links »

| HOME | ABOUT | PRODUCTS | SERVICES |

Business and running partners Suzie Swift and Rose Chu established the first Active Sports Outlet (ASO) at 7600 Kimball Avenue over a decade ago. They realized that most sporting goods retailers at the time were concentrating on adventure sports merchandise — for example, rock climbing and kayaking gear — and Lincoln Park residents with less extreme interests were underserved. Two years after opening the Kimball store, ASO opened a shop at the Lakepoint Galleria. ASO then successfully expanded outside of Lincoln Park. Today, ASO is the top destination exclusively for tennis, cycling, and running enthusiasts across the country.

This year ASO proudly debuted a line of clothing, Active Attire, designed by Olympic sprinter Jess Logan. It is available at all locations and through this Web site. Click Products to view our comfortable and colorful clothing and footwear for men and women.

Note that special services are available exclusively at our original location. These services include bicycle and treadmill reconditioning, tennis racquet re-stringing, and more. Click Services to schedule a repair or to leave an inquiry.

Done 🔒 ● Internet

161. What is indicated about the owners of ASO?
(A) They design sportswear.
(B) They run together.
(C) They are professional cyclists.
(D) They are interested in selling the ASO chain.

162. The word "established" in paragraph 1, line 1, is closest in meaning to
(A) demonstrated.
(B) introduced.
(C) challenged.
(D) furnished.

163. What is suggested about ASO?
(A) It does not sell adventure sports gear.
(B) It does not own any stores outside of Lincoln Park.
(C) It no longer sells its products online.
(D) It no longer operates a store in the Lakepoint Galleria.

GO ON TO THE NEXT PAGE.

MADISON, February 20 – On February 18, the Madison City Council approved new regulations relating to street vendors. As the number of tourists has increased in recent years, street vendors selling everything from tacos to hand-made jewelry have also become more numerous. The new regulations will limit the number of street vendors permitted to operate within each business district and establish rules about where street vendors can locate their carts.

Street vendors will be required to purchase a six-month permit that will allow them to sell their goods only within a certain area of the city. The city will provide only a limited number of permits in each district. The permits will cost $100 and must be clearly displayed on each cart. Applications for vendor permits must be made in person at the city safety office on University Avenue between March 1 and May 30. The regulations will require street vendors to keep a minimum distance of 50 feet from each other. The new regulations will take effect on March 15 of this year.

164. The word "certain" in paragraph 2, line 2, is closest in meaning to
(A) Positive.
(B) Profitable.
(C) Dependable.
(D) Specific.

165. What is NOT stated about the new permits?
(A) They cost $100.
(B) They must be visible.
(C) They are available immediately.
(D) They are valid for six months.

166. What is the new minimum distance between vendor carts?
(A) 5 feet.
(B) 10 feet.
(C) 50 feet.
(D) 100 feet.

167. What is implied in the article?
(A) Street vendors are currently not permitted to sell food.
(B) The city council anticipates that few vendors will not apply for permits.
(C) There has previously been no limit on the number of street vendors.
(D) Applications for permits may be submitted by mail.

City of El Paso
Department of Revenue
Commissioner Andrea Juarez
1 Commerce Plaza
El Paso, TX 79901

Dear Mr. Diaz,

Congratulations! Your application for a building permit has been approved and enclosed with this letter. Please be reminded that the permit must be displayed in a prominent location where the work is taking place, and be clearly visible to inspectors.

Now that you have received your building permit, please visit our Web site (http://www.elpaso.gov/index) to complete and submit the appropriate tax form electronically. Once approved (the process takes less than 10 minutes) you are **authorized** to collect taxes. Please be aware that if you do not file a business tax form within 15 days of receiving your permit, you will be ordered to pay a fine of $500 per day, and your license may be suspended for up to 10 business days, or until the tax form is filed.

Thank you for doing business in the city of El Paso. If you still need some help or have questions, feel free to give us a call at 915-234-1880.

Sincerely
Andrea Juarez
Commissioner of Revenue

---

168. What information is announced in the letter?
(A) A license has been issued.
(B) A fine was imposed in error.
(C) An office has been moved.
(D) A new tax law has been passed.

169. What does Ms. Juarez ask Mr. Diaz to do?
(A) Pay a processing fee.
(B) Contact a local office.
(C) Approve a request.
(D) Submit a form.

170. In the second paragraph, line 3, the word "authorized" is closest in meaning to
(A) undecided.
(B) organized.
(C) purchased.
(D) empowered.

171. Which of the following is NOT mentioned in the letter?
(A) Instructions for displaying the license.
(B) Possible penalties for failure to submit a form.
(C) The type of business owned by Mr. Diaz.
(D) Ms. Juarez's official title.

GO ON TO THE NEXT PAGE.

POSITION INFORMATION	MONOLITH FINANCIAL CORP.
	EMPLOYMENT APPLICATION

Position(s) desired:	Senior accountant, corporate accounts department

Position preferred (please mark preference):	Permanent: X̲ Full-Time: X̲ Part-Time: X̲ Temporary: __

APPLICANT INFORMATION	Note: (A) Applicants must supply contact information for three professional references at time of the interview. (B) Applicants who are seeking a part-time position will not be entitled to a benefits package (Health and life insurance; paid leave for illness; retirement; bonuses).

Last name:	Cooper	Address:	
First name:	Henry	7960 Williams Drive	
Middle initial:	T.	Clarendon Hills, IL 60514	
		Phone:	Home: (708) 323-6055
			Work: (312) 910-0032

QUALIFICATIONS & EDUCATION

School or college attended, degree obtained:	Markham Institute of Economics University of Illinois - Finance, BA University of Chicago - Accounting, MS American Institute of Certified Public Accountants – CPA

EMPLOYMENT HISTORY	
Current employer:	Leonard Stein & Associates, Chicago, IL
Title and length of time:	Accountant, 3 years
Supervisor(s), name and title:	Larry Fine, manager, Corporate Accounting Division Geraldine Markowitz, director, Human Resources Department
Your Duties (please be specific):	I have analyzed and continue to assist in the maintenance of the accounting system. I review tax statements and advise on tax preparations. This year, I have also been a training consultant with the Human Resources Department.

172. What position does the applicant desire?
   (A) Manager.
   (B) Consultant.
   (C) Accountant.
   (D) Counselor.

173. Who submitted the application form?
   (A) Henry Cooper.
   (B) Leonard Stein.
   (C) Larry Fine.
   (D) Geraldine Markowitz.

174. What type of employment will the applicant likely NOT accept?
   (A) Full-time.
   (B) Part-time.
   (C) Long-term.
   (D) Short-term.

175. According to the form, when will the applicant be required to submit additional information?
   (A) When reporting for work.
   (B) When giving financial advice.
   (C) When accepting the position.
   (D) When meeting the employer.

GO ON TO THE NEXT PAGE.

Questions 176-180 refer to the following schedule and e-mail.

Olivia Vargas – Itinerary – October 21-26

THE STAPLETON GROUP

MONDAY
9:00 A.M
Marketing team meeting
1:15 P.M.
Lunch meeting with Bart DeNozzio
4:00 P.M.

TUESDAY
9:00 A.M.
Executive Staff monthly meeting
10:45 A.M
Review budgets with department managers
2:40 P.M.
Train departs for Baltimore, arrival 4:45 P.M.

WEDNESDAY
9:15 A.M.
Meet with Rosedale office team to plan upcoming advertising campaign
1:00 P.M.
Return to Philadelphia, arrival 2:05 P.M.
5:30 P.M.
Prepare for Quarterly Board Meeting

THURSDAY
8:30 A.M.
Breakfast meeting with Leslie Pinder (legal team)
1:45 P.M.
Meet with Adrienne McLain and her campaign director
4:30 P.M.
Quarterly Board Meeting

FRIDAY
8:00 A.M
New York conference call
10:00 A.M
Meet with IT to go over Web site revisions
2:00 P.M.
Meet to review video campaign
5:30 P.M.
London office conference call

Profit International LLC

HQ
The Stapleton Building
100 5th Avenue
New York, NY 10019

Phone: (212) 440-2299
www.stapletongroup.com

From:	Ken Kash<k_kash@stapletongroup.com>
To:	Olivia Vargas <o_vargas@stapletongroup.com>
Re:	Daily Update
Date:	October 22

✉ Palace Garden Comfirmation Email 18k

Dear Ms. Vargas,

Here are some quick updates regarding your schedule this week.

First, the legal team supervisor has a conflict on Thursday morning and asked to postpone that meeting to early next week instead. I can fill that morning slot with Terry Greer, the graphic designer whose resume you liked. You wanted to interview him about potential work on the RedJet campaign. Please let me know whether I should call him to make the arrangement.

Also, Desmond Byers from the CEO's office has confirmed that he will be joining the meeting on Friday to go over the video campaign. I have booked the multi-media room for that meeting as you requested.

Finally, since you'll be traveling today, I am sending as an attachment a copy of the e-mail from the Palace Garden Hotel confirming your reservation. I think you already have the train ticket and a detailed itinerary. Let me know if you didn't receive them, and I can send them electronically.

Ken Kash

176. What electronic file is sent with the e-mail?
(A) A hotel confirmation.
(B) A board meeting itinerary.
(C) Train tickets.
(D) Digital photographs.

177. What action does Mr. Kash ask about?
(A) Reviewing legal documents.
(B) Contacting a designer.
(C) Approving a marketing campaign.
(D) Sending an updated resume.

178. Who has asked to change a meeting time?
(A) Ms. Pinder.
(B) Mr. Anders.
(C) Mr. DeNozzio.
(D) Ms. McLain.

179. At what time will Ms. Vargas and Ms. Byers attend a meeting on Friday?
(A) 8:00 A.M.
(B) 10:00 A.M.
(C) 2:00 P.M.
(D) 5:30 P.M.

180. What is suggested about the Stapleton Group?
(A) It has more than 50 staff members.
(B) It is the largest marketing campaign to Australia.
(C) It opened within the last year.
(D) It has offices in several cities.

GO ON TO THE NEXT PAGE.

From:	Irene Wooley <I_Wooley@LoebandBunson.com>
To:	Sibena Tarik <Tarik1503@zifmall.com>
Re:	Account manager position
Date:	Thursday, April 6 12:05 p.m.

Dear Ms. Tarik,

My colleague and I enjoyed meeting you at our offices yesterday. We were very impressed with your presentation about multimedia advertising and we would like to continue the conversation further. We are inviting all finalists for the account manager position back to our office for a second round of interviews.

As I told you earlier, the new account manager will be part of the home appliance division headed by Mr. Robertson. He would like to hear your ideas about advertising as well as give you a sense of the culture and the way we do business at Loeb & Bunson. If you are available next Friday, April 14, we would to see you again here in our Burlington office. Alternatively, we could meet with you here the following Monday (April 17).

Please contact me or my assistant, Ms. Jefferson, to make arrangements at your earliest convenience. We look forward to seeing you again.

Sincerely,
Irene Wooley
Personnel Director
Loeb & Bunson

From:	Sibena Tarik <Tarik1503@zifmall.com>
To:	Irene Wooley <I_Wooley@LoebandBunson.com>
Re:	Account manager position
Date:	Friday, April 7 9:13 a.m.

Dear Ms. Wooley,

I was pleased to hear from you about the account manager position. I am still very much interested in the position at your advertising firm, and I would be happy to talk with you and your colleagues further about my ideas and experience here at Ultrasonic Advertising. Unfortunately, I already have plans to make a presentation at a conference in Concord on the first day that you proposed, but I can certainly come to your offices on April 17.

Also, as a follow-up to my interview this week, I have asked Mr. Derek Smalls, my supervisor in my current position, to send a letter of reference on my behalf. If you would like to see more samples of my work before or during my visit, please let me know. I look forward to seeing you.

Sincerely,

Sibena Tarik

181. What is the purpose of the first e-mail?
(A) To advertise a new product.
(B) To assign a project.
(C) To schedule an interview.
(D) To make a job offer.

182. What type of business is Loeb & Bunson?
(A) A publishing company.
(B) An accounting firm.
(C) An advertising firm.
(D) An appliance company.

183. When is Ms. Tarik planning to be at a conference?
(A) On April 6.
(B) On April 7.
(C) On April 14.
(D) On April 17.

184. According to the first e-mail, why does Mr. Robertson want to meet Ms. Tarik?
(A) To introduce her to some members of his team.
(B) To acquaint her with the company's style and expectations.
(C) To discuss her upcoming presentation.
(D) To provide her with travel information.

185. Who is NOT an employee of Loeb & Bunson?
(A) Ms. Wooley.
(B) Mr. Smalls.
(C) Mr. Robertson.
(D) Ms. Jefferson.

GO ON TO THE NEXT PAGE.

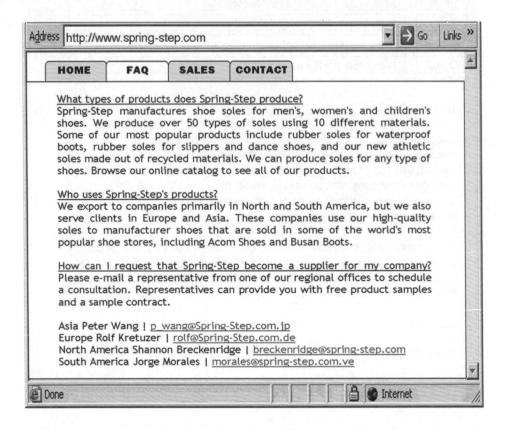

From:	Joana Nunez <nunez@spring-step.com.ar>
To:	Daniel Talbot <director@lambada.com.br>
Re:	FWD: Consultation query
Date:	September 9

Dear Mr. Talbot,

I'm Joana Nunez, the new South American regional representative. Your message was forwarded to me by Ms. Breckenridge.

On behalf of Spring-Step, I would like to thank you for expressing interest in our products. I'm sorry that you had difficultly reaching a representative.

We are currently in the midst of a modest corporate restructuring and I'm afraid that Mr. Jorge Morales is no longer with the company. From this point forward, I will be handling all vendor consultations.

In response to your query, after viewing your Web site, it appears that our synthetic soles are similar to the ones you are currently using. Second, I would be happy to provide you with a wide range of samples, as well as discuss your vendor options. Please respond with a detailed list of the types of soles you'd like to sample and include your shipping address. Meanwhile, if you wish to speak directly with me, I can be reached at +35 382 83488.

I look forward to hearing from you.

Regards,

186. What is indicated about Spring-Step?
(A) It manufactures athletic shoes.
(B) It makes products primarily intended for children.
(C) It ships its products to multiple countries.
(D) It sends its clients a monthly catalog.

187. What is most likely true about Ms. Breckenridge?
(A) She works for Lambada S.A.
(B) She can send the free samples to potential clients.
(C) She has traveled to Brazil.
(D) She met Mr. Talbot in Miami.

188. What type of materials does Mr. Talbot most likely want to use for his company's products?
(A) Recycled.
(B) Synthetic.
(C) Rubber.
(D) Organic.

189. Who did Mr. Talbot first attempt to contact?
(A) Mr. Wang.
(B) Ms. Nunez.
(C) Ms. Breckenridge.
(D) Mr. Morales.

190. How did Ms. Breckenridge respond to Mr. Talbot's email?
(A) She deleted it.
(B) She replied directly.
(C) She forwarded it to an associate.
(D) She sent a copy to everyone in the company.

GO ON TO THE NEXT PAGE.

Joyful String Quartet

CONTACT: John Hartman
PHONE: 510-532-0339
EMAIL: john@joyfulstrings.org
WEBSITE:
http://www.joyfulstrings.org

FOR IMMEDIATE RELEASE

[TOUR DATES ANNOUNCED]
JSQ SOUTHEAST SUMMER TOUR

CHARLESTON, South Carolina, March 21

The Joyful String Quartet, the region's oldest string quartet, has announced the dates of its summer tour. The six-date tour will include a performance at the historic Beacon Theater in Atlanta, where JSQ first appeared in concert twenty years ago.

Scheduled performances are as follows.

Date	City – Location
June 10	Charleston, SC – Marion Opera House
June 13	North Charleston, SC – The North Charleston Performing Arts Center
June 16	Hilton Head Island, SC – The Sea Pines Pavilion
June 18	Savannah, SC – Glenmorris Ballroom
June 22	Augusta, GA – Imperial Amphitheater
June 25	Atlanta, GA – Beacon Theater

Tickets, which range from $15 for balcony seats to $40 for center-section seats on the orchestra level for all tour dates, are now avaliable at venue box offices and online ticket retailers. Members of the recently established Joyful String Quartet Fan Club will receive a 15% discount on tickets purchased with their member ID number through the exclusive members' link on www.joyfulstrings.org.

A full list of fan club privileges and an explanation of annual dues can be found on www.joyfulstrings.org/fanclub_membership.

THE SEA PINES PAVILLION
HILTON HEAD ISLAND, SC

 Q Prime

FOR IMMEDIATE RELEASE
MAY 25
PRESS OFFICE: 812-909-3330
CONTACT: ALLEN FROST
http://www.seapines.com

Cancelled and Postponed Performances

HILTON HEAD ISLAND, South Carolina - Effective immediately, most live performances scheduled for the month of June have been postponed because of emergency repair work on the pavilion band shell.

Ticket holders are encouraged to retain their tickets, with the exception of the Joyful String Quartet concert; most shows will be rescheduled for later dates, and tickets for the June performances will be honored. For the most current information on the rescheduling of the performances. visit The Sea Pines Pavilion Web site, www.seapines.com

To request a refund for the canceled Joyful String Quartet concert, please contact Allen Frost at 812-909-3330 or frost@seapines.com

The Sea Pines Pavilion
1 Sea Plantation Way
Hilton Head, SC 43372

Phone: 812-SEA-PINE
Fax: 812-384-0007
http://www.seapines.com

GO ON TO THE NEXT PAGE

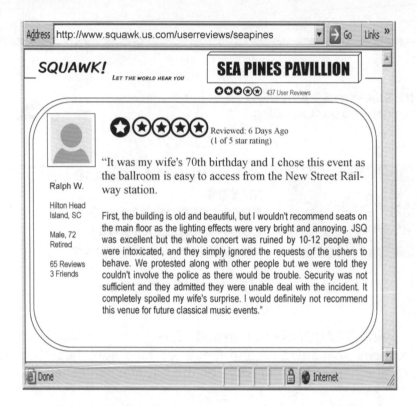

SQUAWK! *LET THE WORLD HEAR YOU*

SEA PINES PAVILLION

✪✪✪✪✪ 437 User Reviews

✪✪✪✪✪ Reviewed: 6 Days Ago
(1 of 5 star rating)

Ralph W.

Hilton Head
Island, SC

Male, 72
Retired

65 Reviews
3 Friends

"It was my wife's 70th birthday and I chose this event as the ballroom is easy to access from the New Street Railway station.

First, the building is old and beautiful, but I wouldn't recommend seats on the main floor as the lighting effects were very bright and annoying. JSQ was excellent but the whole concert was ruined by 10-12 people who were intoxicated, and they simply ignored the requests of the ushers to behave. We protested along with other people but we were told they couldn't involve the police as there would be trouble. Security was not sufficient and they admitted they were unable deal with the incident. It completely spoiled my wife's surprise. I would definitely not recommend this venue for future classical music events."

Done | Internet

191. What is suggested about the Joyful String Quartet Fan Club?
(A) Its members receive discounts at Gallica Music stores.
(B) Its members are asked to pay a fee every year.
(C) It was established over twenty years ago.
(D) It meets every year in the month of June.

192. What is mentioned about tickets for the Joyful String Quartet's concerts?
(A) They are discounted for students who show their school identification card.
(B) They are sold exclusively through online ticketing agents.
(C) They cost slightly more than they did for last year's tour.
(D) They are the same price for balcony seating at each concert venue.

193. Where did the Joyful String Quartet play its first concert two decades ago?
(A) In Charleston.
(B) In Atlanta.
(C) In Savannah.
(D) In Augusta.

194. When will the Joyful String Quartet NOT be expected to perform a scheduled concert?
(A) On March 1.
(B) On May 25.
(C) On June 16.
(D) On June 22.

195. According to the user review, what spoiled the concert for the man and his wife?
(A) The musicians were out of tune.
(B) The staff was rude.
(C) Some audience members were disruptive.
(D) Some parts of the performance were too loud.

From:	Monica Montague <m.montague@sunsetcoop.com>
To:	Brian Pierson <brian.pierson@thriftyprint.com>
Re:	T-Shirt Order #TP-9986
Date:	October 9

Dear Mr. Pierson,

As activity coordinator for Sunset Cooperative Elementary School, I recently placed an order for 400 T-shirts printed with our school logo. I specified that we wanted the shirts in four different colors in equal numbers.

When we unpacked the shirts, however, we discovered that 200 were green, 100 were blue, and 100 were yellow. The red shirts were missing and we received twice the number of green shirts we expected.

We require four different colors to represent the four different teams in our school's annual fall festival, so we still need 100 red shirts. Is it possible for us to have them by October 22 so that our teams can wear them for our festival that day?

This is an important tradition for us, so we really need to have them by then.

Thank you,

Monica Montague
Activity Coordinator, Sunset Cooperative

From:	Brian Pierson <brian.pierson@thriftyprint.com>
To:	Monica Montague <m.montague@sunsetcoop.com>
Re:	T-Shirt Order #TP-9986
Date:	October 9

Dear Ms. Montague,

I have reviewed our records and agree that Thrifty Print has made an error.

Correcting your order is our top priority. We will print your red t-shirts right away and send them via express service tomorrow (October 10). You should receive them by October 12 at the latest. If you would like to keep the extra green shirts, you can buy them at our wholesale cost of $3.75 per shirt. If you have no need for them, send them back to us. We will credit your account for the cost of the return shipping.

Thrifty Print truly regrets the problem with your order. Please accept a gift of 400 pencils in colors and quantities matching your original T-shirt order, customized with your school's logo. Perhaps you can give them as prizes at the festival. They will be included in the express shipment. We appreciate your business and will do what we can to keep it!

Regards,
Brian Pierson
Owner, Thrifty Print

GO ON TO THE NEXT PAGE

5th Annual Fall Festival

Sunset Cooperative is delighted to be hosting its Fifth Annual Fall Festival.

Our past festivals have established a proud tradition in which the school and the local community come together to celebrate and enjoy a memorable day of entertainment with rides, games, music, and more.

Admission to the Fall Festival will be $5. The fun starts at 11:00 a.m. and ends? Come early and stay late!

Highlights

- In addition to a carnival-style atmosphere, the festival features another tradition; the Tug-of-War tournament. This year we will have four teams competing against each other for the grand prize!

SUNSET COOPERATIVE ELEMENTARY SCHOOL

1234 Kirkham Street at the corner of 46th Avenue

Monica Montague: 415-334-0099

Time: 11:00 a.m. until ???

Date: Saturday, October 22

SFUSD

196. Why does the school need T-shirts in several colors?
- (A) To offer as prizes for different contests at a festival.
- (B) To consider as replacements for existing uniforms.
- (C) To give students more choices for purchase.
- (D) To distinguish different groups in the school from each other.

197. What does Ms. Montague ask Mr. Pierson to do?
- (A) Exchange red T-shirts for blue t-shirts.
- (B) Send the red T-shirts she ordered.
- (C) Correct the logo on some red T-shirts.
- (D) Double the quantity of her original T-shirt order.

198. When will shirts be worn?
- (A) On April 9.
- (B) On April 12.
- (C) On April 22.
- (D) On October 22.

199. For what does Mr. Pierson offer to pay?
- (A) The cost of designing a logo.
- (B) The cost of returning items she ordered.
- (C) The cost of printing on some.
- (D) The cost of hosting an event.

200. The T-shirts are most likely intended for what purpose?
- (A) The Tug-of-War tournament.
- (B) The local volunteer staff.
- (C) Teachers and parents.
- (D) Friends and neighbors.

Stop! This is the end of the test. If you finish before time is called, you may go back to Parts 5, 6, and 7 and check your work.

GO ON TO THE NEXT PAGE

New TOEIC Listening Script

PART 1

1. (　　) (A) Some people are working in a restaurant.
        (B) Some people are working in a factory.
        (C) Some people are riding a bus.
        (D) Some people are painting a wall.

2. (　　) (A) A woman is walking a dog.
        (B) A woman is pushing a shopping cart.
        (C) A woman is driving a car.
        (D) A woman is paying for her purchases.

3. (　　) (A) The man is carrying a box.
        (B) The man is sitting down.
        (C) The man is shoveling snow.
        (D) The man is working on a computer.

4. (　　) (A) The priest is giving a sermon.
        (B) The doctor is performing surgery.
        (C) The officer is writing a ticket.
        (D) The firefighter is unrolling a hose.

5. (　　) (A) Many bicycles are on the rack.
        (B) Many boats are in the harbor.
        (C) Many cars are stuck in traffic.
        (D) Many airplanes are in the sky.

6. (　　) (A) They are climbing up a mountain.
        (B) They are climbing down the stairs.
        (C) They are crossing a stream.
        (D) They are boarding a plane.

PART 2

7. (   ) Is the conference room ready to go for our meeting with Mr. Brown?
   (A) Yes, it's all set.
   (B) Yes, they were on time.
   (C) Yes, he asked for it yesterday.

8. (   ) Would you like to use the copier or should I turn it off when I'm done?
   (A) I'll buy a used one.
   (B) I really like it.
   (C) Turn it off, please.

9. (   ) Would you like to attend a seminar for restaurant managers?
   (A) It depends on when it is.
   (B) He was promoted recently.
   (C) A hundred and twenty five dollars.

10. (   ) The Burnside Overpass is going to be closed for construction next week, isn't it?
   (A) Yes, we're open until nine.
   (B) It's going fine, thank you.
   (C) Yes, and the following week as well.

11. (   ) When is Ms. Teller due to arrive?
   (A) That's what I suggested.
   (B) On platform B.
   (C) Any minute now.

12. (   ) Where's the nearest ATM?
   (A) You can borrow mine.
   (B) Down the street, next to the post office.
   (C) It has more variety.

13. (   ) Who's supposed to write the article on stock market trends?
   (A) I think John is.
   (B) It's on the left.
   (C) Please print it out again.

14. (   ) Would you like a map of the park?
   (A) I did already.
   (B) At a garage.
   (C) Sure, it might come in handy.

GO ON TO THE NEXT PAGE.

15. (　　) This is the latest issue of the magazine, isn't it?
        (A) I think you still have time.
        (B) No, on the cover.
        (C) Yes, it just came out.

16. (　　) When will the career fair be over?
        (A) Yes, it's over there.
        (B) They're quite different.
        (C) In about half an hour.

17. (　　) When are you planning to arrive at the Christmas party?
        (A) He came here last year.
        (B) Unfortunately, I can't go.
        (C) I brought one, too.

18. (　　) Do you have a moment to proofread my report?
        (A) Sorry, I don't.
        (B) Usually on weeknights.
        (C) Many charts and graphs.

19. (　　) Didn't you say you were a vegan?
        (A) Yes, but don't make it too salty.
        (B) As a matter of fact, my whole family is.
        (C) Fresh fruits and vegetables.

20. (　　) Will you be available at 10 o'clock?
        (A) How about 11:30?
        (B) No, I haven't.
        (C) Is that right?

21. (　　) Where do I submit my expense forms?
        (A) My trip to Singapore.
        (B) It's too much.
        (C) The accounting department.

22. (　　) I ordered several boxes of doughnuts for Wednesday's morning meeting.
        (A) The tables are in the corner.
        (B) Just the board members.
        (C) I think that should be plenty.

23. (   ) Why are you moving to Oklahoma City?
        (A) In two days.
        (B) A long walk.
        (C) For a new job.

24. (   ) Do you offer health insurance for all full-time workers?
        (A) Gloves and a hard hat.
        (B) Yes, after 60 days.
        (C) At the manufacturing facility.

25. (   ) Weren't you expecting more people to come to the safety seminar?
        (A) I received it yesterday.
        (B) No, this is everybody.
        (C) In the auditorium.

26. (   ) Would you like to call the customer back or should I do it?
        (A) I shouldn't have done that.
        (B) Yes, I've seen that one.
        (C) Let me take care of it.

27. (   ) When will we release the updated software?
        (A) They're in the accounting department.
        (B) At least seven.
        (C) It's too early to tell.

28. (   ) The Smoke Hut serves great Kansas City-style barbecue.
        (A) Isn't it kind of expensive?
        (B) Next to the theater.
        (C) I presented it to a few colleagues.

29. (   ) Why isn't Joshua working on the Web site launch?
        (A) On the front page.
        (B) I thought he was.
        (C) Next Friday.

30. (   ) How do I dial an outside number from the office phone?
        (A) Press 2 then wait for a dial tone.
        (B) I rented in downtown Denver.
        (C) Call me after three.

GO ON TO THE NEXT PAGE.

31. (　　) We can afford to hire more full time staff, can't we?
        (A) Yes, they were.
        (B) It was discounted.
        (C) I'll review the budget.

PART 3

Questions 32 through 34 *refer to the following conversation.*

M: You know, I'm having trouble concentrating in my cubicle. It gets quite noisy in this part of the office. The break room is just around the corner. And on Fridays they have big meetings in the conference room next door.

W: Have you inquired about telecommuting? You might be able to do your work from home some of the time. Management is slowly coming around to the concept. I've started doing that once in a while. Sometimes it's just more convenient.

M: Oh, really. That would make my Fridays much more productive. I'll ask my manager about it.

32. (　　) What is the man concerned about?
        (A) Rising paper costs.
        (B) Noise in the office.
        (C) A parking area closure.
        (D) Poor mobile phone reception.

33. (　　) What does the woman suggest?
        (A) Using public transport.
        (B) Working from home.
        (C) Reschedule a meeting.
        (D) Finding a different supplier.

34. (　　) What does the man say he will do?
        (A) Contact a supervisor.
        (B) Go on a trip.
        (C) Assemble a team.
        (D) Participate in a training session.

Questions 35 through 37 *refer to the following conversation.*

W : I'd like to reserve a table for three on the evening of May 24th, please. Are there any tables available in the first seating?

M : Yes, I have one table for three at 5:30 p.m.

W : Oh, that's too early. Is there anything a little later? I'm meeting some clients at the airport at 5:00. With traffic, there's no way we can be there by 5:30.

M : Well, I could hold the table for you until 5:45. Would that give you enough time? Otherwise, I have tables available starting at 7:30.

35. (   ) What is the woman inquiring about?
   (A) A payment option.
   (B) A ticket upgrade.
   (C) A flight schedule.
   (D) A dinner reservation.

36. (   ) What does the woman say she needs to do at 5:00 p.m.?
   (A) Give a presentation.
   (B) Rent a hotel room.
   (C) Meet some clients.
   (D) Catch a connecting flight.

37. (   ) What does the man say he can do?
   (A) Cancel a reservation.
   (B) Take a later flight.
   (C) Hold a table.
   (D) Contact a client.

Questions 38 through 40 _refer to the following conversation between three speakers._

W : This is Joanna from research and development in the Brook Building. We were supposed to get a package from the Scranton laboratory last week, but it never arrived.

American M : Hang on a second. Hey, Tony! Did we receive a package from Scranton? It's Joanna from R and D.

AUS M : No. I haven't seen anything.

American M : OK, Tony says he hasn't seen anything. If you give me the tracking number, I can check our database. That will tell us if it's in the system and still in transit.

W : It's 7-2-2-1-G-T. By the way, I was told by the technician that the package is bright red and has a shiny green logo on the side. That would certainly distinguish it from the plain brown boxes we usually receive.

American M : Thanks for that information. As soon as I find out your package's whereabouts, I'll let you know.

GO ON TO THE NEXT PAGE

38. (   ) What is the purpose of the call?
   (A) To purchase some supplies.
   (B) To return some merchandise.
   (C) To make shipping arrangements.
   (D) To locate a missing item.

39. (   ) What does American M ask for?
   (A) A tracking number.
   (B) An inventory amount.
   (C) The location of a building.
   (D) The weight of package.

40. (   ) What does the woman say about the box?
   (A) It is larger than average.
   (B) It may have been damaged.
   (C) It is needed soon.
   (D) It is brightly colored.

Questions 41 through 43 _refer to the following conversation._

W : Hi, I'm Tiffany Campbell from Third Eye Design Magazine. I'm here to interview the director
    of the gallery.
M : Oh, you're a bit early, aren't you, Ms. Campbell? Mr. Grover isn't back from lunch yet.

W : Actually, I purposely came early because I'd like to look around and take a few photographs
    for the article before I meet with Mr. Grover, if that's okay.
M : Sure, feel free to look around. And here's the gallery map. It shows you the plan for both
    the first and second floors.

41. (   ) Who most likely is the woman?
   (A) A journalist.
   (B) A caterer.
   (C) An architect.
   (D) A receptionist.

42. (   ) What does the woman say she wants to do while she waits?
   (A) Attend a lecture.
   (B) Take some photos.
   (C) See a special exhibit.
   (D) Have lunch.

43. (   ) What does the man give the woman?
     (A) A free membership.
     (B) An audio recording.
     (C) A floor plan.
     (D) A daily schedule.

Questions 44 through 46 *refer to the following conversation.*

M : Good afternoon. Welcome to the Brookfield farmer's market. Would you like to try some of our homegrown olives?

W : Thank you. They're delicious. But I wanted to buy some tomatoes. I remember you had plenty this time last year.

M : Actually, we're just getting ready to start picking the tomatoes now. We should have some at the market next week if you'd like to come back then.

44. (   ) Where are the speakers most likely to be?
     (A) At a food market.
     (B) At a restaurant.
     (C) At a department store.
     (D) At a bank.

45. (   ) What does the man offer the woman?
     (A) A sample.
     (B) A menu.
     (C) A newsletter.
     (D) A shopping bag.

46. (   ) According to the man, what will happen next week?
     (A) Job applications will be accepted.
     (B) An item will become available.
     (C) Prices will be lowered.
     (D) A new location will open.

Questions 47 through 49 *refer to the following conversation.*

M : Do you have any plans for lunch?

W : Yes, I do! I've been invited to a luncheon by some associates from the sales department.

M : Where are you meeting them?

W : Red's House of Prime Rib.// I can't wait!//

GO ON TO THE NEXT PAGE.

M : Wow! That's pricey for a Tuesday afternoon luncheon, isn't it?

W : Well, it's sort of a celebration. We recently closed a deal with Marcum Manufacturing. The V.P. of sales is picking up the tab, I guess.

M : I was going to say, who's paying? By the way, why did they invite you? Did you play a part in closing the deal?

W : As a matter of fact, I crunched all the numbers in the contract proposal.

47. (   ) What does the woman mean when she says, "I can't wait!"?
      (A) She is late for an appointment.
      (B) She is running out of patience.
      (C) She is excited about the event.
      (D) She is reluctant to speak.

48. (   ) What is the occasion for the luncheon?
      (A) To make a presentation.
      (B) To celebrate a business deal.
      (C) To honor a retiree.
      (D) To introduce new employees.

49. (   ) What does the woman say?
      (A) She led the team that gave the proposal.
      (B) She had nothing to do with the proposal.
      (C) She played an important part in the proposal.
      (D) She will not be present at the proposal.

Questions 50 through 52 *refer to the following conversation.*

W : OK, your purchase comes to a total of sixty-seven dollars and twenty cents, sir. Do you have a preferred shopper's card for our store?

M : No, I don't. This store is very convenient for me. I live just two streets away. I've never heard of the preferred shopper's card, and I'm surprised no one told me about it before.

W : Well, it's a rewards card. If you enroll in the program, you get points for every dollar you spend here. When you earn fifty points you'll get a coupon for one of the products you buy most often. Here's a form you can fill out to get started.

50. (   ) Who most likely is the woman?
      (A) A bank employee.
      (B) A security guard.
      (C) A marketing consultant.
      (D) A shop cashier.

51. (   ) What does the man say about the business?
      (A) It has a good selection.
      (B) It has convenient hours.
      (C) It has weekly discounts.
      (D) It is close to his home.

52. (   ) What does the woman suggest the man apply for?
      (A) A contest.
      (B) A loan.
      (C) An employment opportunity.
      (D) A shopper rewards card.

Questions 53 through 55 *refer to the following conversation.*

W : Good afternoon, Dr. Dylan. I'm calling to confirm your progress on the product testing. You're scheduled to bring some participants in to test the new disposable contact lenses today, right?

M : Well, we weren't able to recruit enough participants yet. We tried to recruit ten people but only five were available. So we postponed the testing until next week.

W : Okay, that's not a problem. But could you get me the results as soon as possible when you're finished? I need the report by the end of next week.

M : Of course, I was planning to do that. I'll make sure you'll have the report by Thursday.

53. (   ) What are the speakers mainly discussing?
      (A) An advertising idea.
      (B) A hiring decision.
      (C) A product test.
      (D) A recent sale.

54. (   ) What problem does the man mention?
      (A) A business is closed.
      (B) An invoice listed the incorrect amount.
      (C) An event was delayed.
      (D) An order was shipped on the wrong date.

55. (   ) What does the man agree to do by Thursday?
      (A) Turn in a report.
      (B) Revise a manual.
      (C) Create an agenda.
      (D) Give a presentation.

GO ON TO THE NEXT PAGE.

M : OK, ma'am. Your total comes to exactly $380. Will you be paying with cash or credit?

W : Here's my Visa card. Oh wait – I have a discount coupon. I'm pretty sure it's still valid. Where is it? There it is.

M : Great, thanks. Hmm, looks like the scanner isn't accepting the bar code. Let me see what the problem is.

W : I know what it is. Would you mind if I leave these items here while I browse the store for another item?

M : Certainly. I'll set these shirts aside, and they'll be here when you're ready to check out.

56. (   ) What is the man doing?
   (A) Assisting a customer.
   (B) Handing out coupons.
   (C) Arranging some displays.
   (D) Restarting a computer.

57. (   ) Look at the graphic. Why was the coupon rejected?
   (A) It has expired.
   (B) It was issued by another store.
   (C) It must be approved by a manager.
   (D) It is for purchases of $400 or more.

58. (   ) What does the man agree to do?
   (A) Hold some items at the counter.
   (B) Initialize the coupon.
   (C) Authorize an additional discount.
   (D) Call another staff member.

W : Hi, I reserved a standard room at your hotel for this Friday, but I'd like to make an upgrade. Are there any suites available that night?

M : I'm sorry, but we have a two-night minimum for our largest rooms. Would you be interested in staying an additional night, either Thursday night or Saturday night?

W : Hmm, I'd love to, but I'm only staying one night for the computer convention at McCormick Place.

M : Well, let me check with my manager then. He might be able to waive the restrictions since you'll be here for the convention.

59. (   ) Why is the woman calling the hotel?
　　　　(A) To organize a conference.
　　　　(B) To confirm an address.
　　　　(C) To complain about a service.
　　　　(D) To change a reservation.

60. (   ) What does the man suggest?
　　　　(A) Taking a shuttle bus.
　　　　(B) Checking the hotel's website.
　　　　(C) Calling back at a later time.
　　　　(D) Staying an additional night.

61. (   ) What will the man ask the manager to do?
　　　　(A) Explain a policy.
　　　　(B) Provide a schedule.
　　　　(C) Authorize a discount.
　　　　(D) Change a restriction.

Questions 62 through 64 _refer to the following conversation._

M : I'm Ed from Ultra Construction. I'm here because you called earlier to request service. There's some kind of foul odor, right?

W : Thanks for coming on such short notice. The odor has been coming from the meeting room ceiling since a week ago or so. You can see a large stain, right there.

M : You probably have a dead critter in there, but I'll have to get some tools and supplies and come back tomorrow to get into the ceiling.

W : That's fine. I'd just like to have this taken care of before Monday. I'm conducting a workshop then so I'll have to be able to use the room.

GO ON TO THE NEXT PAGE.

62. (　　) Why was the man's company contacted?
        (A) To build a garage.
        (B) To investigate a bad smell.
        (C) To remove a tree.
        (D) To install an appliance.

63. (　　) What does the man say he will do before returning tomorrow?
        (A) Pick up supplies.
        (B) Test some equipment.
        (C) Hire extra workers.
        (D) Talk to a manager.

64. (　　) What will the woman do on Monday?
        (A) Call the man.
        (B) Host an event.
        (C) Paint a room.
        (D) Send a payment.

Questions 65 through 67 _refer to the following conversation and notice._

W : Ray, there's a new concert series opening at the Regal Auditorium and some of us from work are planning to go. Are you interested?

M : Sure, I've read about the series. Sounds like there's going to be a lot of great music. How much are tickets?

W : It depends. Look, here's the information. We already have more than ten people committed to attending, so we should qualify for that price.

M : That's certainly reasonable. Would that be for this weekend?

W : Yes, after work on Friday.

M : Is someone going to order the tickets in advance?

W : Lou in the marketing department is. You could give him a call and let him know to include you.

65. (　　) What type of event are the speakers discussing?
        (A) A theater performance.
        (B) A museum exhibit opening.
        (C) A photography workshop.
        (D) A live music concert.

66. (   ) Look at the graphic. What ticket price will the speakers probably pay?
  (A) $15.
  (B) $18.
  (C) $20.
  (D) $25.

> ### REGAL AUDITORIUM
> ### Admission Price (per Person)
>
> University student $18
> Group of 10 or more $20
> Member $15
> Nonmember $25

67. (   ) What does the woman suggest the man do?
  (A) Pay with a credit card.
  (B) Rent some equipment.
  (C) Leave work early.
  (D) Call a coworker.

Questions 68 through 70 *refer to the following conversation and invoice.*

W : Will that be all for today? Just a new phone and service upgrade?

M : I do have one more question before I buy the phone. Can I pay my bill online? I travel a lot for work and I'm not at home when the bills come.

W : Absolutely. You can set up a payment account on our website. I also recommend downloading a mobile phone application so you can view the status of your account anytime.

M : OK, great. But I think I changed my mind about the extended warranty. I don't think I really need it. Could you remove that from my bill?

W : Of course.

68. (   ) Who most likely is the woman?
  (A) A store clerk.
  (B) A real estate agent.
  (C) A banker.
  (D) A teacher.

GO ON TO THE NEXT PAGE.

69. (   ) What does the man ask about?
    (A) Additional features.
    (B) Online payments.
    (C) Trade-in policies.
    (D) Coverage area.

70. (   ) Look at the graphic. How much will be removed from the bill before taxes?
    (A) $75.00.
    (B) $76.56.
    (C) $100.
    (D) $700.

Frazier Mobile		
Billing Statement: 06/23		
www.fzrmobile.com		
Equipment	FZR 9980 Silver 16GB GSM	$700.00
Service Plan	Diamond Unlimited (monthly)	$75.00
Warranty	Two-year Extended	$100.00
Sub-total		$875.00
Fees and Taxes/State sales tax (8.75%)		$76.56
Total		$951.56

PART 4

**Questions 71 through 73** refer to the following talk.

Good morning, ladies and gentlemen, and welcome to this introductory session on using our new restaurant management software. Today we're going to get familiar with the basic features you'll need when you're on the floor as a server. We'll go over how to order menu items, generate guest bills and process payments, and manage your end of shift tasks. I think this new software will save you a lot of time when taking care of our diners. I know we had problems with our old software crashing frequently. The new program is much more stable.

71. (　　) Who are the listeners?
  (A) Software developers.
  (B) Legal assistants.
  (C) Restaurant staff.
  (D) Hotel managers.

72. (　　) What will the listeners do at the workshop?
  (A) Develop goals for the upcoming year.
  (B) Discuss customer feedback.
  (C) Learn to use new software.
  (D) Participate in role-playing activities.

73. (　　) What does the speaker expect will happen?
  (A) Customers will write positive reviews.
  (B) Sales volumes will increase.
  (C) There will be fewer billing errors.
  (D) Employees will work more efficiently.

Questions 74 through 76 refer to the following telephone message.

Hello Ms. Louganis, this is Derek Sharper from Sharper Realty. I'm calling to set up an appointment for you to see a loft apartment that's just become available in the Garment District. I think this property would be perfect for you. It's the largest in the building and is zoned for commercial and residential use. I'd be happy to show you this property anytime tomorrow or before noon on Monday. Please call me back and let me know when you're available for a showing.

74. (　　) Where does the speaker most likely work?
  (A) At a real estate agency.
  (B) At a law firm.
  (C) At an insurance policy.
  (D) At a warehouse.

75. (　　) What does the speaker say about the property?
  (A) It has modern facilities.
  (B) It is in a good location.
  (C) It is large.
  (D) It is not available.

GO ON TO THE NEXT PAGE.

76. (   ) What does the speaker ask the listener to do?
   (A) Visit a Web site.
   (B) Make an appointment.
   (C) Apply for a loan.
   (D) Return a phone call.

Questions 77 through 79 _refer to the following broadcast._

As new workers in the production department here at Samuk Shoes, you will be spending most of your time in the assembly areas we've just visited. But it's a good idea for us to see the rest of the facilities as well. This way you have an idea of where the other departments are located and the functions they serve. Our first stop will be the shipping department. To access the warehouse and dock areas, you'll need to swipe your security badge at the gate. So please have that ready.

77. (   ) Who is the intended audience for the talk?
   (A) Customers.
   (B) Job candidate.
   (C) Production workers.
   (D) Managerial staff.

78. (   ) According to the speaker, where will the listeners go next?
   (A) To the assembly floor.
   (B) To the shipping department.
   (C) To a training room
   (D) To a security office.

79. (   ) What are the listeners asked to do?
   (A) Practice safety procedure.
   (B) Sign a form.
   (C) Turn in a job application.
   (D) Use a security badge.

Questions 80 through 82 _refer to the following news report._

Vestige Entertainment, North America's largest game manufacturer announced that it's delaying the release of its popular computer game, Combat Engagement 2, until next spring. Speaking at a press conference this morning, Vestige's CEO Louis Maher said the latest version of Combat Engagement will not go on sale until additional product testing is completed. After testing is finished and the game is released, it is expected to sell out quickly, so the customers are being advised to place their orders early.

80. (   ) What type of business is Vestige Entertainment?
    (A) A game developer.
    (B) An electronic store.
    (C) A weapons manufacturer.
    (D) A wedding planner.

81. (   ) Why is there a delay?
    (A) Some materials are not available.
    (B) Machinery is being replaced.
    (C) A price has not been determined.
    (D) More product testing is necessary.

82. (   ) What are customers encouraged to do?
    (A) Order items in advance.
    (B) Check a Web site for updates.
    (C) Compare specifications.
    (D) Read consumer reviews.

Questions 83 through 85 *refer to the following talk and map.*

Welcome to the new volunteer orientation at the Williams Wildlife Rescue Center. We're happy that you'll be guiding our wildlife tours. Behind me is a trail map of the rescue center. We're now walking down the Lincoln Trail and we'll pass the raptors and the bats before heading toward the aquatic center. You can use the other trails as well, except for this trail right here because there's a troop of chimpanzees living nearby. For the first time, the center's collaborating with the state university on a research project about chimps. We've positioned live cameras in the area and we don't want anything to disturb the chimps for the duration of the study.

83. (   ) Who is the talk intended for?
    (A) Nature photographers.
    (B) City officials.
    (C) New volunteers.
    (D) University students.

GO ON TO THE NEXT PAGE.

84. (   ) Look at the graphic. Which trail is closed to visitors?
    (A) North Lincoln Trail.
    (B) Cumberland Trail.
    (C) DeKalb Trail.
    (D) Dawson Trail.

85. (   ) What project is the Center participating in?
    (A) An annual clean-up day.
    (B) A program to plant more trees.
    (C) A series of seminars on wildlife conservation.
    (D) A research study on chimpanzees.

Questions 86 through 88 _refer to the following instructions._

This month all post office employees will be required to attend a customer service workshop. The two-hour session is planned for the evening of Thursday, April 22nd, after regular business hours. If you work part-time, please note that you will be paid for the extra hours. I'm handing out some materials right now which I'd like you to review before the workshop. This is an updated employee handbook that includes some new guidelines on working with the public. We'll discuss the changes in more detail during the workshop.

86. (   ) What will happen on April 22?
    (A) Mail service will be extended.
    (B) Paychecks will be issued.
    (C) A training session will be held.
    (D) Work schedules will be adjusted.

87. (　　) What are listeners asked to review?
   (A) A customs declaration.
   (B) A project timeline.
   (C) A customer survey.
   (D) An employee handbook.

88. (　　) What does the speaker say about the part-time employees?
   (A) They will receive a certificate.
   (B) They will be paid for extra time.
   (C) They are not included in a policy.
   (D) They must sign a tax form.

Questions 89 through 91 *refer to the following announcement.*

Attention shoppers. The Shops at White Oak Village is happy to announce that it's turning five years old. Stores will be opening early tomorrow morning for the start of our anniversary celebration and offering special promotions on their merchandise. Customers can pick up a brochure with discount coupons at our information desk, located on the ground floor across from Vance Jewelry. Be sure to shop early to take advantage of the lowest prices of the year.

89. (　　) What is being announced?
   (A) An anniversary celebration.
   (B) A grand opening.
   (C) A renovation project.
   (D) A sweepstakes giveaway.

90. (　　) What will happen tomorrow morning?
   (A) An award will be presented.
   (B) A restaurant will serve free breakfast.
   (C) Stores will open early.
   (D) A design will be displayed.

91. (　　) According to the announcement, what is available at the information desk?
   (A) A schedule of events.
   (B) A brochure with coupons.
   (C) A map of the area.
   (D) A list of restaurants.

GO ON TO THE NEXT PAGE.

Hey, guys. I know many of you have questions regarding our new advertising contract with Ashley Furniture. I'm afraid I failed to explain myself clearly yesterday, so let me try again. As you know, Ashley's has asked our agency to come up with an ad campaign for their new line of glass and wood coffee tables. This is a very important project, so I'd like the whole team to be involved. I'd like each one of you to sketch a one-page ad showing the table in an attractive light. Then, at our next meeting, you will present your ideas and together we'll choose the most promising one. Does anyone have any questions?

92. (   ) Why has the speaker called today's meeting?
    (A) To discuss the quarterly budget.
    (B) To clarify an assignment.
    (C) To finalize product designs.
    (D) To test a new product.

93. (   ) What has the company been asked to do?
    (A) Design a coffee table.
    (B) Create an advertising campaign.
    (C) Lower monthly costs.
    (D) Meet an earlier deadline.

94. (   ) According to the speaker, what will happen at the next meeting?
    (A) A demonstration will be held.
    (B) A competitor's product will be analyzed.
    (C) Proposals will be reviewed
    (D) Materials will be rewritten.

Hi, Bob, it's Carolyn from accounting. I'm looking at the expense report you submitted for your recent sales trip to Boston and it looks like one of the receipts is missing. I see you're requesting reimbursement for an expense of $45.86 on October 12, but I can't find the receipt for it. It wasn't included with your report. I'll need that to process payment. If you don't have it anymore, give me a call and I'll explain what the procedure is for requesting reimbursement without a receipt.

95. (   ) Why is the speaker calling?
  (A) A meeting has been cancelled.
  (B) A client has a question.
  (C) A flight has been delayed.
  (D) A receipt is missing.

96. (   ) Look at the graphic. Which expense needs to be documented?
  (A) Airfare.
  (B) Restaurant.
  (C) Taxi.
  (D) Hotel.

TRAVEL EXPENSE REPORT

Name: Bob Colvin

Department: Sales

Date(s) of trip: October 12-13

Date	Amount	Description
10/12	$124.00	Round-trip economy class airfare (Phila. – Boston)
10/12	$45.86	Taxi from Boston Logan International to Camp Corp.
10/12	$77.29	Meal with client at Bosco's Restaurant
10/12	$15.50	Certified copies of signed contracts
10/13	$225.00	K Hotel Boston
10/13	$55.93	Taxi from K Hotel Boston to BOS

Total: $487.65

97. (   ) What does the speaker say she can do?
  (A) Explain a process.
  (B) Issue a check.
  (C) Issue a receipt.
  (D) Contact a supervisor.

Questions 98 through 100 refer to the following talk and agenda.

Nice to be here, Leigh. And thanks, everyone, for attending this evening's session of the city council. The main item on our agenda is to address the issue of traffic delays around

GO ON TO THE NEXT PAGE.

the Evergreen Point Bridge. Following the results of a study we conducted in June, a temporary traffic control program was initiated. We posted four police officers to direct traffic entering and exiting the bridge during the morning and evening rush hours. The trial period was a success, and now that it's over, we have to make a decision. We'd like to make this a permanent part of our traffic control program, but this will require additional funding. So I'd like to introduce our city budget director Ingrid Medina, who will explain how we might be able to pay for this new program without raising taxes.

98. (   )   What problem is the speaker addressing?
　　　　　　(A) Scheduling delays.
　　　　　　(B) Road congestion.
　　　　　　(C) Budget cuts.
　　　　　　(D) Tax reductions.

99. (   )   What did the city do in June?
　　　　　　(A) Conducted a study.
　　　　　　(B) Changed parking regulations.
　　　　　　(C) Held an election.
　　　　　　(D) Fired four police officers.

100. (   )   Look at the graphic. Who is the current speaker?
　　　　　　(A) Leigh Brawley.
　　　　　　(B) Tiffany Cheever.
　　　　　　(C) Ingrid Medina.
　　　　　　(D) Scott Rippertin.

CITY OF BELLEVUE
CITY COUNCIL AGENDA
August 23 7:00 p.m.

7:00-7:10   Welcome and introduction – Leigh Brawley, moderator

- Purpose of meeting – Tiffany Cheever, City of Bellevue mayor
- City of Bellevue, Office of Budget and Management – Ingrid Medina, city budget director
- Snohomish County Department of Transportation – Scott Rippertin, acting deputy

7:30-8:30   Public comment and open discussion – Leigh Brawley, moderator

---

NO TEST MATERIAL ON THIS PAGE

GO ON TO THE NEXT PAGE

New TOEIC Speaking Test

Question 1: Read a Text Aloud

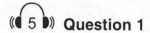 **Question 1**

Directions: In this part of the test, you will read aloud the text on the screen. You will have 45 seconds to prepare. Then you will have 45 seconds to read the text aloud.

The best travel experiences happen when you get off the beaten track, but that doesn't mean all so-called tourist traps are no-nos. While many are overcrowded and underwhelming, a choice few are worth their inherent hassles.

PREPARATION TIME
00 : 00 : 45

RESPONSE TIME
00 : 00 : 45

Question 2: Read a Text Aloud

 **Question 2**

Directions: In this part of the test, you will read aloud the text on the screen. You will have 45 seconds to prepare. Then you will have 45 seconds to read the text aloud.

It's no surprise that the nation's largest cities have the worst traffic, but size alone doesn't automatically mean more delays. Drivers in Phoenix, the largest city with the best traffic flow, have about as much wasted time per year as those in Louisville or San Francisco. And smaller towns don't lack for backups; Nashville and Denver offer as much downtime behind the wheel as Miami and Dallas.

PREPARATION TIME
00 : 00 : 45

RESPONSE TIME
00 : 00 : 45

GO ON TO THE NEXT PAGE

Question 3: Describe a Picture

Directions: In this part of the test, you will describe the picture on your screen in as much detail as you can. You will have 30 seconds to prepare your response. Then you will have 45 seconds to speak about the picture.

PREPARATION TIME
00 : 00 : 30

RESPONSE TIME
00 : 00 : 45

70

Question 3: Describe a Picture

答題範例

 **Question 3**

A woman is sitting on a park bench.

She is reading a magazine.

She is also wearing a hat.

Her bike is parked nearby.

She appears to have gone out for a ride.

Then she decided to take a rest.

There is no one else in the park.

It's a cool fall day.

Judging from the shadows, it's late afternoon.

The bench is made of wood.

It has long slats to sit on.

Park benches are rarely comfortable.

There is a big tree in the background.

It has a very thick trunk.

It is probably a pine tree.

When the woman is done reading, she will get back on her bike.

Maybe she will go visit a friend.

It's a good day to be outdoors.

GO ON TO THE NEXT PAGE.

Questions 4-6: Respond to Questions

 **Question 4**

Directions: In this part of the test, you will answer three questions. For each question, begin responding immediately after you hear a beep. No preparation time is provided. You will have 15 seconds to respond to Questions 4 and 5 and 30 seconds to respond to Question 6.

Imagine that you are participating in a research study about education. You have agreed to answer some questions in a telephone interview.

Question 4

What is your opinion of home schooling?

Question 5

Would you allow your children to be home schooled?

Question 6

What are some of the advantages and disadvantages of home schooling?

Questions 4-6: Respond to Questions

答題範例

 **Question 4**

What is your opinion of home schooling?

Answer

> I guess it's OK.
>
> Some people prefer to learn at home.
>
> I don't have a problem with it.

 **Question 5**

Would you allow your children to be home schooled?

Answer

> Sure.
>
> If they had special needs.
>
> Whatever is best for the children is fine with me.

GO ON TO THE NEXT PAGE

Questions 4-6: Respond to Questions

 **Question 6**

What are some of the advantages and disadvantages of home schooling?

Answer

I think one of the positive aspects is control.

By home schooling, you can monitor your child's progress.

In that way, a parent can be more involved.

Also, it allows the children to go at their own pace.

There are fewer deadlines and due dates.

I think it puts less pressure on the kids.

On the downside, the kids miss out on a social life.

They need to interact with other kids.

They may find it difficult to adjust when it's time to enter

the real world.

Questions 7-9: Respond to Questions Using Information Provided

 **Question 7**

Directions: In this part of the test, you will answer three questions based on the information provided. You will have 30 seconds to read the information before the questions begin. For each question, begin responding immediately after you hear a beep. No additional preparation time is provided. You will have 15 seconds to respond to Questions 7 and 8 and 30 seconds to respond to Question 9.

House for rent
$1,000 per month

4 bedroom, 2 bath house on East Washington Avenue in Escondido – just minutes from downtown San Diego. Home has a brand new kitchen with granite counter tops, new stainless steel appliances, new bathroom sinks and vanities, new custom paint throughout with crown molding and new carpet in the bedrooms. New washer & dryer. 12-inch custom tile floors in kitchen, living room and bathrooms. Two-car garage with utility area. Extra large lot in back of house for parking with security gate in front. 1st and last months rent. Available February 10th. Please contact Jeff @ 858-405-6982.

Hi! This is Jack Steele. I'm calling about the house for rent. Would you mind if I asked a few questions?

PREPARATION TIME
00 : 00 : 30

Question 7

RESPONSE TIME
00 : 00 : 15

Question 8

RESPONSE TIME
00 : 00 : 15

Question 9

RESPONSE TIME
00 : 00 : 30

GO ON TO THE NEXT PAGE

Questions 7-9: Respond to Questions Using Information Provided

答題範例

 **Question 7**

Where is the house located?

Answer

> The house is in Escondido.
>
> It's on East Washington Avenue.
>
> Escondido is about a ten-minute drive from downtown San
>
> Diego.

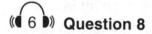 **Question 8**

How many bedrooms and bathrooms does the house have?

Answer

> The house has four bedrooms.
>
> It has two bathrooms.
>
> Both have been recently renovated.

Questions 7-9: Respond to Questions Using Information Provided

 **Question 9**

What are some of the outstanding features of the house?

Answer

Well, first of all, the location is great.

Escondido is a great community.

It's close enough to downtown to be convenient, yet

 quite peaceful and suburban.

The home has a new kitchen with granite counter tops

 and new stainless steel appliances.

The bathrooms have new sinks and vanities.

There is new carpet in the bedrooms.

It also has a new washer & dryer.

There's a two-car garage with a utility area.

And finally, an extra large lot in back of house for parking

 with security gate in front.

GO ON TO THE NEXT PAGE

Question 10: Propose a Solution

 **Question 10**

Directions: In this part of the test, you will be presented with a problem and asked to propose a solution. You will have 30 seconds to prepare. Then you will have 60 seconds to speak. In your response, be sure to show that you recognize the problem, and propose a way of dealing with the problem.

In your response, be sure to

• show that you recognize the caller's problem, and

• propose a way of dealing with the problem.

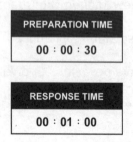

PREPARATION TIME
00 : 00 : 30

RESPONSE TIME
00 : 01 : 00

Question 10: Propose a Solution

答題範例

 **Question 10**

Voice Message

> This is Steve Chen from the power plant construction site in Pittsburgh. I got your memo about the delay in delivering the turbines from our partner in Japan. This is really bad news for the project. We're already two months behind schedule and the board of directors is starting to get very impatient with this. As you maybe realize, a delay in installing the turbines holds up many other parts of the overall construction process. Exactly how long will we need to wait? What should I tell the board? This has put me in a bit of tight spot. Please call me as soon as you get this message. The number is (312)998-3256. Thanks.

GO ON TO THE NEXT PAGE.

Question 10: Propose a Solution

答題範例

Steve,

Julie Froom returning your call.

I've listened to your message and let's see how I can help.

The situation with the turbines is almost resolved.

They've been held up in customs for an unusually long time.

I've just received word that they've finally been cleared for transport.

Within the next day or two, we expect the turbines to be loaded onto

   semi-trucks in L.A.

From there it will be a week before they arrive in Pittsburgh.

I'll email a copy of the bill of lading as soon as I receive it.

I've given some thought to what you might tell the board of directors.

Of course, I completely understand their growing impatience.

Two months behind schedule is unfortunate.

I believe that honesty is the best policy.

Just tell them the truth.

The turbines were inexplicably held up in customs.

To be safe, why not say the turbines will arrive in two weeks.

That way you're covered if there are any delays.

And everyone will be pleasantly surprised if they arrive earlier.

Question 11: Express an Opinion

 **Question 11**

Directions: In this part of the test, you will give your opinion about a specific topic. Be sure to say as much as you can in the time allowed. You will have 15 seconds to prepare. Then you will have 60 seconds to speak.

Some experts are predicting that wind and sea power are the most promising energy sources of the future. Do you agree or disagree, and why?

PREPARATION TIME
00 : 00 : 15

RESPONSE TIME
00 : 01 : 00

GO ON TO THE NEXT PAGE.

Question 11: Express an Opinion

答題範例

 **Question 11**

I agree that natural, renewable energy resources like wind and sea power hold the
  most promise.

Unfortunately, I don't see them being developed to their full potential.

Here's why.

First, oil companies and greedy politicians will never let it happen.

Unless they are able to control the distribution of energy and absorb the profits, they
  will fight to the death to prevent any change in the energy landscape.

They don't care about energy or the environment; they care about money.

Second, average citizens don't know or care where their power comes from.

The only thing they care about is that the light comes on when they flip the switch.

For them, it is much easier to remain ignorant and uninformed.

Meanwhile, the government will be reluctant to develop these resources.

They won't want to cross their buddies who own the oil companies.

They are in cahoots with each other.

Thus, it all boils down to money.

Because wind and sea power are limitless and basically free, it would be almost
  impossible to charge people for them.

The only thing you could charge them for is distribution, and there's not a lot of money
  in that.

In my view, the only way wind and sea power reach their promise is if we run out of oil.

Some experts say that might happen in the next century.

Others say we may never run out of it.

NO TEST MATERIAL ON THIS PAGE

GO ON TO THE NEXT PAGE.

New TOEIC Writing Test

Questions 1-5: Write a Sentence Based on a Picture

Question 1

Directions: Write ONE sentence based on the picture using the TWO words or phrases under it. You may change the forms of the words and you may use them in any order.

couple / formal

Questions 1-5: Write a Sentence Based on a Picture

Question 2

Directions: Write ONE sentence based on the picture using the TWO words or phrases under it. You may change the forms of the words and you may use them in any order.

elephant / ride

GO ON TO THE NEXT PAGE

Questions 1-5: Write a Sentence Based on a Picture

Question 3

Directions: Write ONE sentence based on the picture using the TWO words or phrases under it. You may change the forms of the words and you may use them in any order.

plans / consult

Questions 1-5: Write a Sentence Based on a Picture

Question 4

Directions: Write ONE sentence based on the picture using the TWO words or phrases under it. You may change the forms of the words and you may use them in any order.

woman / cell phone

GO ON TO THE NEXT PAGE.

Questions 1-5: Write a Sentence Based on a Picture

Question 5

Directions: Write ONE sentence based on the picture using the TWO words or phrases under it. You may change the forms of the words and you may use them in any order.

collide / intersection

Questions 6-7: Respond to a written request

Question 6

Directions: Read the e-mail below.

From:	big_bob_boss@gmail.com>
Sent:	Sunday, May 5
To:	girl_fly_22@yahoo.com
Subject:	Writers' group

Debbie,

I had the fortune of stumbling upon your group while searching for writing clubs in Taipei. Any chance you're still taking members? I'm a freelance Chinese-English translator, but I'm also hoping to complete a screenplay by the summer and am scavenging for creative fuel and feedback.

I look forward to hearing from you.

Thanks,
Bob Travis

Directions: Write Bob as the leader of the writing group. Invite him to join the group and give at least (2) two details about the group, i.e. when and where it meets, etc.

GO ON TO THE NEXT PAGE.

Questions 6-7: Respond to a written request

答題範例

Question 6

Bob,

Thanks for inquiring about the Taipei Writers' Group. As it happens, we just had a spot open up and I'd like to invite you to join us. We meet every other Saturday afternoon at Dante's Café near Shida. The meeting begins at 3:00 p.m. and typically last an hour and a half or longer, depending on what material we're discussing.

As for the size of the group, we've found that ten is the most manageable and productive number, but the actual number of writers who submit their work varies from week to week. That way, we have a consistent amount of material coming in, and enough people to give feedback.

Let me know if you decide to accept this invitation and I can give you details about our next meeting.

Yours,
Debbie Knowles

Questions 6-7: Respond to a written request

Question 7

Directions: Read the e-mail below.

From:	Lucy Liu
Sent:	Saturday, April 4
To:	Brian Fishman
Subject:	Parking spot

Brian,

I was very distressed to come home last night and find your car in my parking space - again. To make matters worse, there were no extra spots in the lot and, therefore, I was forced to park two blocks away. And guess what else happened? This morning I discovered my car had been broken into and vandalized.

Despite repeatedly asking you not to park in my spot, you continue to ignore me and do as you please. Perhaps I have been too lenient in allowing you to take advantage of our friendship and my kindness. Those days are over, buddy. I am holding you personally responsible for the damage to my car.

You can expect to hear from my lawyer and I've already filed a complaint with building management. Meanwhile, the next time you park in my spot, your car will be towed.

Yours,

Lucy

Directions: You didn't park in Lucy's spot last night. Give evidence to prove it.

GO ON TO THE NEXT PAGE.

Questions 6-7: Respond to a written request

答題範例

Question 7

Lucy,

First of all, let me say I'm horrified to hear about your car. Yes, I did park in your parking spot, once, over a year ago, after asking for your permission. However, I did not park in your spot last night, mainly because I wouldn't park in your spot without permission, but in reality, I have been in Las Vegas for the last week. In fact, I won't be home until Tuesday.

So I'm really sorry that you've been upset but I didn't have anything to do with it. You do realize that several people in our complex drive black BMW's, don't you? Good luck getting this straightened out, but leave me out of it. Thanks.

Sincerely,
Brian

Questions 8: Write an opinion essay

Question 8

Directions: Read the question below. You have 30 minutes to plan, write, and revise your essay. Typically, an effective response will contain a minimum of 300 words.

Has technology made the world a better place to live? Provide reasons or examples to explain your opinion.

GO ON TO THE NEXT PAGE.

Questions 8: Write an opinion essay

答題範例

Question 8

For starters, I love technology and there is no doubt in my mind that it has made the world a better place. However, technology adversely affected human nature. The majority of us drive cars and these cars are driven on roads that are made to a higher standard and faster than ever before——but there is a price. The price is that many jobs are now obsolete due to the use of machinery and without manual labor we have greater levels of physical inactivity. Higher levels of physical inactivity lead to higher levels of adverse health conditions and this is not isolated only to the development of roads. Every industry you can think of has cut our human labor with highly efficient machines and it is only going to get worse.

The advancement in computer technology and in particular the development of instant information has changed how we communicate and socialize. As adults we have to learn how our children are communicating but it can not be at the expense of basic manners. I was told recently how a mother communicated to her son to "turn the volume down" on the downstairs television through Facebook. This loss of traditional communication can also be seen with groups at a restaurant where most are engaging in mobile phone activity with little talking going on.

Technology is there to make life simpler, but sometimes I wish for the simple life my grandparents told me about. Those were the days when most people had physical activity in their work day and the walk to work was just as good as the $20,000 treadmill we now use at the gym. The days are gone when morning and afternoon tea was a time for robust discussions and laughter rather than writing LOL on text messages even though you have not laughed out loud for months. The days where dinner was served on a plate rather than from a drive-thru window no longer exist.

Now I also know those simple years had there own difficulties but there must be a balance. We are presently in the years of "no balance" and unless we get some "balance," like a human that loses balance, our society will fall down.

TOEIC ANSWER SHEET

REGISTRATION No.

姓名 / NAME

LISTENING SECTION

Part 1

No.	ANSWER A B C D
1	Ⓐ Ⓑ Ⓒ Ⓓ
2	Ⓐ Ⓑ Ⓒ Ⓓ
3	Ⓐ Ⓑ Ⓒ Ⓓ
4	Ⓐ Ⓑ Ⓒ Ⓓ
5	Ⓐ Ⓑ Ⓒ Ⓓ
6	Ⓐ Ⓑ Ⓒ Ⓓ
7	Ⓐ Ⓑ Ⓒ
8	Ⓐ Ⓑ Ⓒ
9	Ⓐ Ⓑ Ⓒ
10	Ⓐ Ⓑ Ⓒ

Part 2

No.	ANSWER A B C D
11	Ⓐ Ⓑ Ⓒ
12	Ⓐ Ⓑ Ⓒ
13	Ⓐ Ⓑ Ⓒ
14	Ⓐ Ⓑ Ⓒ
15	Ⓐ Ⓑ Ⓒ
16	Ⓐ Ⓑ Ⓒ
17	Ⓐ Ⓑ Ⓒ
18	Ⓐ Ⓑ Ⓒ
19	Ⓐ Ⓑ Ⓒ
20	Ⓐ Ⓑ Ⓒ

No.	ANSWER A B C D
21	Ⓐ Ⓑ Ⓒ
22	Ⓐ Ⓑ Ⓒ
23	Ⓐ Ⓑ Ⓒ
24	Ⓐ Ⓑ Ⓒ
25	Ⓐ Ⓑ Ⓒ
26	Ⓐ Ⓑ Ⓒ
27	Ⓐ Ⓑ Ⓒ
28	Ⓐ Ⓑ Ⓒ
29	Ⓐ Ⓑ Ⓒ
30	Ⓐ Ⓑ Ⓒ

Part 3

No.	ANSWER A B C D
31	Ⓐ Ⓑ Ⓒ
32	Ⓐ Ⓑ Ⓒ Ⓓ
33	Ⓐ Ⓑ Ⓒ Ⓓ
34	Ⓐ Ⓑ Ⓒ Ⓓ
35	Ⓐ Ⓑ Ⓒ Ⓓ
36	Ⓐ Ⓑ Ⓒ Ⓓ
37	Ⓐ Ⓑ Ⓒ Ⓓ
38	Ⓐ Ⓑ Ⓒ Ⓓ
39	Ⓐ Ⓑ Ⓒ Ⓓ
40	Ⓐ Ⓑ Ⓒ Ⓓ

No.	ANSWER A B C D
41	Ⓐ Ⓑ Ⓒ Ⓓ
42	Ⓐ Ⓑ Ⓒ Ⓓ
43	Ⓐ Ⓑ Ⓒ Ⓓ
44	Ⓐ Ⓑ Ⓒ Ⓓ
45	Ⓐ Ⓑ Ⓒ Ⓓ
46	Ⓐ Ⓑ Ⓒ Ⓓ
47	Ⓐ Ⓑ Ⓒ Ⓓ
48	Ⓐ Ⓑ Ⓒ Ⓓ
49	Ⓐ Ⓑ Ⓒ Ⓓ
50	Ⓐ Ⓑ Ⓒ Ⓓ

No.	ANSWER A B C D
51	Ⓐ Ⓑ Ⓒ Ⓓ
52	Ⓐ Ⓑ Ⓒ Ⓓ
53	Ⓐ Ⓑ Ⓒ Ⓓ
54	Ⓐ Ⓑ Ⓒ Ⓓ
55	Ⓐ Ⓑ Ⓒ Ⓓ
56	Ⓐ Ⓑ Ⓒ Ⓓ
57	Ⓐ Ⓑ Ⓒ Ⓓ
58	Ⓐ Ⓑ Ⓒ Ⓓ
59	Ⓐ Ⓑ Ⓒ Ⓓ
60	Ⓐ Ⓑ Ⓒ Ⓓ

Part 4

No.	ANSWER A B C D
61	Ⓐ Ⓑ Ⓒ Ⓓ
62	Ⓐ Ⓑ Ⓒ Ⓓ
63	Ⓐ Ⓑ Ⓒ Ⓓ
64	Ⓐ Ⓑ Ⓒ Ⓓ
65	Ⓐ Ⓑ Ⓒ Ⓓ
66	Ⓐ Ⓑ Ⓒ Ⓓ
67	Ⓐ Ⓑ Ⓒ Ⓓ
68	Ⓐ Ⓑ Ⓒ Ⓓ
69	Ⓐ Ⓑ Ⓒ Ⓓ
70	Ⓐ Ⓑ Ⓒ Ⓓ

No.	ANSWER A B C D
71	Ⓐ Ⓑ Ⓒ Ⓓ
72	Ⓐ Ⓑ Ⓒ Ⓓ
73	Ⓐ Ⓑ Ⓒ Ⓓ
74	Ⓐ Ⓑ Ⓒ Ⓓ
75	Ⓐ Ⓑ Ⓒ Ⓓ
76	Ⓐ Ⓑ Ⓒ Ⓓ
77	Ⓐ Ⓑ Ⓒ Ⓓ
78	Ⓐ Ⓑ Ⓒ Ⓓ
79	Ⓐ Ⓑ Ⓒ Ⓓ
80	Ⓐ Ⓑ Ⓒ Ⓓ

No.	ANSWER A B C D
81	Ⓐ Ⓑ Ⓒ Ⓓ
82	Ⓐ Ⓑ Ⓒ Ⓓ
83	Ⓐ Ⓑ Ⓒ Ⓓ
84	Ⓐ Ⓑ Ⓒ Ⓓ
85	Ⓐ Ⓑ Ⓒ Ⓓ
86	Ⓐ Ⓑ Ⓒ Ⓓ
87	Ⓐ Ⓑ Ⓒ Ⓓ
88	Ⓐ Ⓑ Ⓒ Ⓓ
89	Ⓐ Ⓑ Ⓒ Ⓓ
90	Ⓐ Ⓑ Ⓒ Ⓓ

No.	ANSWER A B C D
91	Ⓐ Ⓑ Ⓒ Ⓓ
92	Ⓐ Ⓑ Ⓒ Ⓓ
93	Ⓐ Ⓑ Ⓒ Ⓓ
94	Ⓐ Ⓑ Ⓒ Ⓓ
95	Ⓐ Ⓑ Ⓒ Ⓓ
96	Ⓐ Ⓑ Ⓒ Ⓓ
97	Ⓐ Ⓑ Ⓒ Ⓓ
98	Ⓐ Ⓑ Ⓒ Ⓓ
99	Ⓐ Ⓑ Ⓒ Ⓓ
100	Ⓐ Ⓑ Ⓒ Ⓓ

READING SECTION

Part 5

No.	ANSWER A B C D
101	Ⓐ Ⓑ Ⓒ Ⓓ
102	Ⓐ Ⓑ Ⓒ Ⓓ
103	Ⓐ Ⓑ Ⓒ Ⓓ
104	Ⓐ Ⓑ Ⓒ Ⓓ
105	Ⓐ Ⓑ Ⓒ Ⓓ
106	Ⓐ Ⓑ Ⓒ Ⓓ
107	Ⓐ Ⓑ Ⓒ Ⓓ
108	Ⓐ Ⓑ Ⓒ Ⓓ
109	Ⓐ Ⓑ Ⓒ Ⓓ
110	Ⓐ Ⓑ Ⓒ Ⓓ

No.	ANSWER A B C D
111	Ⓐ Ⓑ Ⓒ Ⓓ
112	Ⓐ Ⓑ Ⓒ Ⓓ
113	Ⓐ Ⓑ Ⓒ Ⓓ
114	Ⓐ Ⓑ Ⓒ Ⓓ
115	Ⓐ Ⓑ Ⓒ Ⓓ
116	Ⓐ Ⓑ Ⓒ Ⓓ
117	Ⓐ Ⓑ Ⓒ Ⓓ
118	Ⓐ Ⓑ Ⓒ Ⓓ
119	Ⓐ Ⓑ Ⓒ Ⓓ
120	Ⓐ Ⓑ Ⓒ Ⓓ

No.	ANSWER A B C D
121	Ⓐ Ⓑ Ⓒ Ⓓ
122	Ⓐ Ⓑ Ⓒ Ⓓ
123	Ⓐ Ⓑ Ⓒ Ⓓ
124	Ⓐ Ⓑ Ⓒ Ⓓ
125	Ⓐ Ⓑ Ⓒ Ⓓ
126	Ⓐ Ⓑ Ⓒ Ⓓ
127	Ⓐ Ⓑ Ⓒ Ⓓ
128	Ⓐ Ⓑ Ⓒ Ⓓ
129	Ⓐ Ⓑ Ⓒ Ⓓ
130	Ⓐ Ⓑ Ⓒ Ⓓ

Part 6

No.	ANSWER A B C D
131	Ⓐ Ⓑ Ⓒ Ⓓ
132	Ⓐ Ⓑ Ⓒ Ⓓ
133	Ⓐ Ⓑ Ⓒ Ⓓ
134	Ⓐ Ⓑ Ⓒ Ⓓ
135	Ⓐ Ⓑ Ⓒ Ⓓ
136	Ⓐ Ⓑ Ⓒ Ⓓ
137	Ⓐ Ⓑ Ⓒ Ⓓ
138	Ⓐ Ⓑ Ⓒ Ⓓ
139	Ⓐ Ⓑ Ⓒ Ⓓ
140	Ⓐ Ⓑ Ⓒ Ⓓ

Part 7

No.	ANSWER A B C D
141	Ⓐ Ⓑ Ⓒ Ⓓ
142	Ⓐ Ⓑ Ⓒ Ⓓ
143	Ⓐ Ⓑ Ⓒ Ⓓ
144	Ⓐ Ⓑ Ⓒ Ⓓ
145	Ⓐ Ⓑ Ⓒ Ⓓ
146	Ⓐ Ⓑ Ⓒ Ⓓ
147	Ⓐ Ⓑ Ⓒ Ⓓ
148	Ⓐ Ⓑ Ⓒ Ⓓ
149	Ⓐ Ⓑ Ⓒ Ⓓ
150	Ⓐ Ⓑ Ⓒ Ⓓ

No.	ANSWER A B C D
151	Ⓐ Ⓑ Ⓒ Ⓓ
152	Ⓐ Ⓑ Ⓒ Ⓓ
153	Ⓐ Ⓑ Ⓒ Ⓓ
154	Ⓐ Ⓑ Ⓒ Ⓓ
155	Ⓐ Ⓑ Ⓒ Ⓓ
156	Ⓐ Ⓑ Ⓒ Ⓓ
157	Ⓐ Ⓑ Ⓒ Ⓓ
158	Ⓐ Ⓑ Ⓒ Ⓓ
159	Ⓐ Ⓑ Ⓒ Ⓓ
160	Ⓐ Ⓑ Ⓒ Ⓓ

No.	ANSWER A B C D
161	Ⓐ Ⓑ Ⓒ Ⓓ
162	Ⓐ Ⓑ Ⓒ Ⓓ
163	Ⓐ Ⓑ Ⓒ Ⓓ
164	Ⓐ Ⓑ Ⓒ Ⓓ
165	Ⓐ Ⓑ Ⓒ Ⓓ
166	Ⓐ Ⓑ Ⓒ Ⓓ
167	Ⓐ Ⓑ Ⓒ Ⓓ
168	Ⓐ Ⓑ Ⓒ Ⓓ
169	Ⓐ Ⓑ Ⓒ Ⓓ
170	Ⓐ Ⓑ Ⓒ Ⓓ

No.	ANSWER A B C D
171	Ⓐ Ⓑ Ⓒ Ⓓ
172	Ⓐ Ⓑ Ⓒ Ⓓ
173	Ⓐ Ⓑ Ⓒ Ⓓ
174	Ⓐ Ⓑ Ⓒ Ⓓ
175	Ⓐ Ⓑ Ⓒ Ⓓ
176	Ⓐ Ⓑ Ⓒ Ⓓ
177	Ⓐ Ⓑ Ⓒ Ⓓ
178	Ⓐ Ⓑ Ⓒ Ⓓ
179	Ⓐ Ⓑ Ⓒ Ⓓ
180	Ⓐ Ⓑ Ⓒ Ⓓ

No.	ANSWER A B C D
181	Ⓐ Ⓑ Ⓒ Ⓓ
182	Ⓐ Ⓑ Ⓒ Ⓓ
183	Ⓐ Ⓑ Ⓒ Ⓓ
184	Ⓐ Ⓑ Ⓒ Ⓓ
185	Ⓐ Ⓑ Ⓒ Ⓓ
186	Ⓐ Ⓑ Ⓒ Ⓓ
187	Ⓐ Ⓑ Ⓒ Ⓓ
188	Ⓐ Ⓑ Ⓒ Ⓓ
189	Ⓐ Ⓑ Ⓒ Ⓓ
190	Ⓐ Ⓑ Ⓒ Ⓓ

No.	ANSWER A B C D
191	Ⓐ Ⓑ Ⓒ Ⓓ
192	Ⓐ Ⓑ Ⓒ Ⓓ
193	Ⓐ Ⓑ Ⓒ Ⓓ
194	Ⓐ Ⓑ Ⓒ Ⓓ
195	Ⓐ Ⓑ Ⓒ Ⓓ
196	Ⓐ Ⓑ Ⓒ Ⓓ
197	Ⓐ Ⓑ Ⓒ Ⓓ
198	Ⓐ Ⓑ Ⓒ Ⓓ
199	Ⓐ Ⓑ Ⓒ Ⓓ
200	Ⓐ Ⓑ Ⓒ Ⓓ

新制多益全真模擬試題③

主　　　編 / 劉　毅

發 行 所 / 學習出版有限公司　　　☎ (02) 2704-5525

郵 撥 帳 號 / 05127272 學習出版社帳戶

登 記 證 / 局版台業 2179 號

印 刷 所 / 文聯彩色印刷有限公司

台 北 門 市 / 台北市許昌街 10 號 2 F　　☎ (02) 2331-4060

台灣總經銷 / 紅螞蟻圖書有限公司　　☎ (02) 2795-3656

本公司網址　www.learnbook.com.tw

電 子 郵 件　learnbook@learnbook.com.tw

售價：新台幣一百八十元正

2017 年 5 月 1 日初版